# STRANGERS
## in town

Ross Macdonald (Kenneth Millar), ca. 1962
(Photograph by Hal Boucher)

# STRANGERS in town

### THREE NEWLY DISCOVERED MYSTERIES BY
# ROSS MACDONALD

## EDITED BY TOM NOLAN

Crippen & Landru Publishers
Norfolk, Virginia
2001

ISBN (limited edition): 1-885941-51-X

ISBN (trade edition): 1-885941-52-8


FIRST EDITION

10 9 8 7 6 5 4 3 2 1


Crippen & Landru Publishers
P. O. Box 9315
Norfolk, VA 23505
USA

Email: CrippenL@Pilot.Infi.Net
Web: www.crippenlandru.com

For Eleanor Van Cott,
Harris Seed, and Norman Colavincenzo

— Tom Nolan

# ACKNOWLEDGMENTS

All quotations from unpublished letters and other unpublished materials by Kenneth Millar and from unpublished letters by Margaret Millar are used with the extremely kind permission of the trustee of the Margaret Millar Charitable Remainder Unitrust, owner of the books, copyrights, and materials related to the collected works of Kenneth Millar (Ross Macdonald) and Margaret Millar.

Permissions to quote materials from cited archives, collections, and libraries have been granted by the University of Michigan, the University of California, Irvine, Indiana University, Columbia University, and Princeton University.

# TABLE OF CONTENTS

✗

Introduction by Tom Nolan ✗ 11

Death by Water ✗ 55

Strangers in Town ✗ 83

The Angry Man ✗ 119

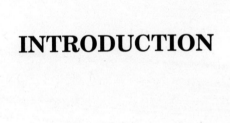

**INTRODUCTION**

# INTRODUCTION

... the reading of detective stories is simply a kind of vice that, for silliness and minor harmfulness, ranks somewhere between smoking and crossword puzzles ... With so many fine books to be read, so much to be studied and known, there is no need to bore ourselves with this rubbish.

Edmund Wilson, "Who Cares Who Killed Roger Ackroyd?" *The New Yorker*, January 20, 1945

I will now confess, in my turn, that, since my first looking into this subject last fall, I have myself become addicted, in spells, to reading myself to sleep with Sherlock Holmes ... I propose, however, to justify my pleasure ... My contention *is* that Sherlock Holmes is literature ... by virtue of imagination and style.

Edmund Wilson, " 'Mr. Holmes, They Were the Footprints of a Gigantic Hound,' " *The New Yorker*, February 17, 1945

Literary critics like Edmund Wilson might feel the need in 1945 to justify an interest in detective fiction, but Ensign Kenneth Millar — an English-criticism doctoral candidate who'd left the University of Michigan to serve as a U.S. Naval officer in World War Two — had no such cultural qualms.

Millar had been enjoying crime tales since childhood — along with shelvesful of classic and contemporary literature, nonfiction, poetry, psychology and philosophy. A brilliant intellect and an aesthetic democrat, Ken Millar savored (and saw the links that connected) the best of all creative efforts, from Kierkegaard to the Keystone Kops.

While still at Michigan, Millar (an A plus graduate

student) put aside his doctoral dissertation on the psychological criticism of Samuel Taylor Coleridge to write in a month (and sell to Dodd, Mead) the domestic spy thriller *The Dark Tunnel*, a tale the Saturday Review's mystery critic judged one of the "books that poked their heads above the fog of a murky" 1944 and "the best 'suspense' yarn of the year."

Ensign Millar (whose *Tunnel* came out as he began Naval duty) didn't plan to return to the university after the war. He intended to make his living as a freelance writer, a scheme much encouraged by his wife Margaret Millar, who by 1945 had herself (with her husband's extensive assistance) produced six well-received mystery novels.

In the three decades after *The Dark Tunnel*, Kenneth Millar (via a three-stage pseudonym) would become known internationally as Ross Macdonald, author of eighteen books featuring private investigator Lew Archer: works a *New York Times* reviewer would call "the finest series of detective novels ever written by an American."

Macdonald would also publish in those years nine Lew Archer short stories, mainly "novelettes" 10- to 15,000 words long, all tailored for specific periodicals. "Most of them were written in a hurry to keep the wolf from the door," the author later said of these Archer shorts, "and not one of them belongs with my mature work."

Nonetheless, genre critics rank Macdonald's short stories among the best modern hard-boiled tales. While the author was right in thinking they weren't on the same level of art as his novels, these shorts have a vivid immediacy that continues to speak strongly to readers. More than mere vehicles to earn quick cash, the short stories gave compelling alternate glimpses of Lew Archer at work in postwar California: that "endless city" stretching from the Mexican border nearly to Oregon.

And it was in the short-story form that Millar first found

the private-eye voice through which he would tell nearly all of his novels.

This volume prints for the first time three previously unpublished Millar/Macdonald private-eye stories: Kenneth Millar's 1945 tale "Death by Water" (the second and final case of one Joe Rogers, private investigator), John Ross Macdonald's 1950 Lew Archer novelette "Strangers in Town," and Ross Macdonald's 1955 Archer story "The Angry Man."

All are arguably as good as Macdonald's published novelettes.  Millar's reasons for not wanting these stories printed were professional, not aesthetic.

"Death by Water" employed a murder-method Millar felt too similar to that of another story he'd written.  "Strangers in Town" was withdrawn when the author wanted to use its plot elements for a Lew Archer novel.  "The Angry Man" was also held back to  provide scaffolding for a book.

Today these stories read as crisply as when they were crafted, and they suggest their eras with an authenticity no newly-written pieces could.

**✗ ✗ ✗**

The place Macdonald's stories evoke so effectively is California, a region inextricably linked to Ross Macdonald's fiction and to Kenneth Millar's identity.

Though brought up in Canada, Millar was born (in 1915) in Los Gatos, California, near San Francisco.  Throughout his childhood, he was reminded he was by birth a U.S. citizen; and the mother who raised him (virtually on her own) spoke often of California as a golden land where Kenneth by rights belonged, and where she hoped he'd return.

It was no whim that had Ensign Millar request, after completing communications training at Boston and Princeton in 1944, to be assigned in early '45 to the 11th Naval District headquarters in San Diego, the city his parents had lived in a year before his birth.  In traveling "back" to California, Millar prepared himself psychologically to come into his own, as an American citizen and as an artist.

"I felt as if a very long, long circle had been completed," Millar later said of his wartime journey to the West Coast. "... I got a tremendous thrill coming in on the Santa Fe train over the great ridge that divides California from Arizona, and coming down across the green summery land that stretches out towards the Pacific. I can't say I felt as if I was coming home, but I felt as if I had perhaps arrived in a place where I wanted to live."

Accompanying the 29-year-old Millar on the Santa Fe Grand Canyon Limited were his wife Margaret and their five-year-old daughter Linda. Both grownup Millars felt an instant sense of déjà-vu in southern California, a place they "knew" from dozens of Hollywood movies. The three Millars stayed for a month (courtesy of the U.S. Navy) at the Cabrillo Hotel in La Jolla, a beautiful oceanfront town they fell in love with. La Jolla immediately became a key point of Ken Millar's imagination; it would be the fictional setting for several Macdonald books. The strongwilled Margaret Millar declared right away she would make Southern California their home; soon she'd start trekking the coast in search of a house to rent or buy.

Margaret and Kenneth Millar would both come into their own as writers in California, though Kenneth's greatest success would take years, while Margaret's was just around the corner. Their mutual immersion in California culture began in La Jolla, where they were befriended by Max Miller, author of the bestselling book *I Cover the Waterfront*. (Within a year, Max Miller would be near-neighbors in La Jolla with Raymond Chandler, a California novelist both Millars greatly admired.)

In February 1945, Ensign Millar was assigned to duty aboard the *U.S.S. Shipley Bay*, an aircraft carrier in the south

Pacific. But his exposure to cultural influence (Californian and otherwise) continued: through first-run Hollywood movies shown aboard ship, through live and recorded music, and through the books and magazines Millar read voraciously. In his isolated weeks at sea, Ken Millar was awash in all sorts of culture, from popular to mainstream to "mandarin." It all helped shape his own creative vision at this crucial juncture.

Millar admired the best art, high and low. The range of his appreciation can be seen in lines he wrote one of his Michigan professors from the *Shipley Bay:* "The Pacific bears some resemblance just now to Dante's non-spatial heaven, and I to a disembodied spirit speaking from the void. I like the place I'm haunting, though; the chow is good, the work is interesting and my fellow-spirits very helpful, I have a book by Andre Gide out of the ship's library, and the nightly movie tonight is 'My Favorite Blonde,' with Bob Hope ..."

The *Shipley Bay* had a good lending library (Millar was thrilled to find his wife's *Fire Will Freeze* on hand); and Margaret mailed additional volumes to Ken. Among works Millar read in February and March of 1945 were Virginia Woolf's *To the Light House* ("a work of almost insane penetration into human relations," Ken commented to Margaret, in one of the near-daily letters they exchanged for almost a year, "and especially the nature of love and of vanity, which is love's little brother"), Mark Twain's *Huckleberry Finn* ("still a masterpiece"), Irving Stone's *Lust for Life* ("no masterpiece"), John Steinbeck's *Tortilla Flat* ("often amusing but a leetle arty"), Oliver Onions' *The Beckoning Fair One* ("far and away the best horror story I have ever read"), Checkhov's *The Hollow*, Edmund Pearson's *Studies in Murder*, Lewis Carroll's *Alice in Wonderland*, Thurber and White's *Is Sex Necessary?*, the sonnets of Shakespeare, and "The Song of Solomon."

Sitting out on deck in the tropics, Millar got sunburned

reading John O'Hara's *Butterfield 8*. Drinking four beers and four whiskey sours in a ramshackle officers' club on some Pacific outpost, he "had a riproarious time" reading Agatha Christie's *The Hazelmoor Mystery:* "A singularly dull book, I thought; even alcohol couldn't stimulate more than a faint interest in it ... Yeah, I figured out the Agatha in the first chapter, but then she wrote it way back in 1931. I remember seeing it when it came out in a magazine that year; I also remember how much better it seemed then ..."

Among the nightly movies Millar saw aboard ship in the spring of 1945 were *The Woman in the Window*, *Together Again* with Charles Boyer and Irene Dunne ("a stinker"), *The Guest in the House* ("the first really good movie I've seen on board ... really psychologico-shivery"), *Belle of the Yukon* with Gypsy Rose Lee ("so bad it was practically good") — and *Double Indemnity*, from the book by Millar favorite James M. Cain, with a script by Billy Wilder and Raymond Chandler ("really first class").

Bombarded by such stimuli, it wasn't long before Millar's own creative urge was aroused. On March 12 he wrote his wife he was "playing around with ideas for stories. I mean short stories, which interest me more right now than anything else." By March 17 he'd written "The Homecoming," a mainstream short about a serviceman returning to his wife. It was set in San Diego, since, as Millar told Margaret, these days "the only place I imagine with automatic ease is Southern California."

Without pause he began plotting two novels, one a wartime spy-story and the other a "psychological love-story" about a Navy survivor and a nurse. He took the spy-story for an OK to his commanding officer, who told him to run the plot past a Navy public relations man.

Partly Millar was moved to action by a letter from his Dodd, Mead editor, hoping Millar would be able to work up a book or two even while at sea. Also encouraging must have been an unexpected query forwarded from a Beverly Hills agent wanting to represent *The Dark Tunnel* for movie sale, and Millar for movie-writing. "No doubt it doesn't mean much," Ken shrugged to Margaret of the agent's letter, "but I liked getting it, and ... if I wasn't otherwise occupied I'd certainly have a try at it."

Soon Millar reported that "the successor to *Tunnel* ... is taking shape (in my head)." On March 24 he wrote Margaret excitedly, "I couldn't go to sleep last night for dreaming up my new thriller plot ... I think it has the old nightmare quality — it should have, I got it in a nightmare practically ..." By March 28 he'd written ten pages of *The Long Ride*, a novel whose story he admitted was "somewhat outlandish but it should do. The main thing is the action, which shifts from Oahu to Detroit to San Diego and Tia Juana ... The long ride occurs on the Grand Canyon Limited, naturally, and also stands for death, also for the ride this guy was taken for, see? Maybe it has sexual implications, too."

Also sparking Millar's creativity this week was a finished copy of his wife's latest book, *The Iron Gates*, which he received aboard ship in late March; he immediately sat down and re-read "treasured bits" of it. Margaret had gotten a $500 advance for this manuscript, whose working title had been "The Skull Beneath the Skin." Her publisher Random House thought highly of the work; they packaged it handsomely and planned to promote it aggressively, not as a mystery but as "a novel of suspense." Their campaign would lead to important reviews, good sales, and favorable reprint deals. A movie deal seemed likely. Her husband urged Margaret to make her next book even better than *Gates:* "In the light of what you've done in less than five years, your possibilities seem practically limitless." Ken enumerated some qualities he thought Margaret Millar's writing and personality had in common: "Honesty so profound it makes you continually unhappy, and so much spirit you are literally younger now than when I met you ... (I long since set myself the definite task of keeping up with you ...)"

Besides his wife, the writer who most immediately inspired Ken Millar was Raymond Chandler, whose four detective books he'd read with intense pleasure. The second of these, *Farewell, My Lovely* (1940), had just been filmed as *Murder, My Sweet*, with Dick Powell starring as Chandler's private-eye hero Philip Marlowe. Ken Millar broke away from writing *The Long Ride* to watch *Murder, My Sweet* on the *Shipley Bay* screen the night of March 30. He loved what he saw. It wasn't as good as the Chandler-coscripted *Double Indemnity*, he thought, but he would *enjoy* it more than any other movie he'd see on ship.

"[I]f Chandler ever brings out another (book) —" Millar wrote Margaret, "which is doubtful since he can do the same stuff for Hollywood at 10 times the price — be sure to send it to me — he's the only one that carries me away — you don't count: *you'd* carry me away if you couldn't write your name."

After that Marlowe movie, the following weeks' cinema fare seemed mostly pathetic to Millar: *Experiment Perilous* ("a stinker"), *Jungle Woman* ("a bum B picture (or C)"), *Orchestra Wives* with Glenn Miller ("I lasted about 20 minutes"), *Spotlight Scandals* ("a prime stinker"), *The Conspirators* with Hedy Lamarr ("surely the world's most passive actress"), Betty Grable in *Footlight Serenade* ("ghastly"), and *The Falcon in Hollywood* ("at which I lasted ... just five minutes, just long enough to spot the killer").

More consistently pleasurable (and often, it seemed, more conducive to creativity) was the time Ken Millar spent on ship listening to music: on records, over Armed Services radio, and occasionally in person. One of his shipmates, Millar reported to Margaret, "plays a fairly hot clarinet. Every now and then he contrives to form a small jazz ensemble in the wardroom, which makes music of a kind. I've been hearing some good music at work ... over the radio: whole programs of Ellington, Waller, Lena Horne, Cole Porter, Charlie Barnet ..." (A yeoman onboard actually knew Porter, who sent him advance copies of his songs.) One of the "Negro stewards" who served the *Shipley Bay*'s officers in the mess had jazz records which Ensign Millar sometimes spent an hour "down the hall" listening to: a Fats Waller version of "Ain't Misbehavin' " that the Millars had in their own collection, " 'Don't Cry Baby,' " some Ellingtoniana, some very hot stuff by Jack Teagarden and a small group including a vocalist called Peggy Lee who is very veddy good." Listening to these discs made Millar feel "extremely nostalgic" for Margaret, he told her: "It's all mixed up with sex ... I think writing is too ... a high form of mental masturbation ..."

His love of writing and of music came together in early April when Millar took a break from working on his manuscript to dash off lyrics to "The Stateside Blues," a song he urged amateur-pianist Maggie to put music to; he was sure it had commercial potential.

Freed from the confines of the university and away from the demands of civilian life, Ken Millar's writing impulse expressed itself in all sorts of ways. In April he started a children's book, *Seabag*, about the *Shipley Bay* captain's dog, to be illustrated by a young lieutenant on board ("I'd not be averse to doing a series with him – in my spare time"). He sent Margaret detailed notes on how to adapt *The Iron Gates* as a play; and he concocted a plot for a book he thought she should write, *The Waiting House* ("big slick material").

All this, as well as the hundreds of letters to Margaret and others, Millar did in-between his shipboard duties, which were fairly demanding.

Ensign Millar was responsible for all coding on the *Shipley*

*Bay*. One of his jobs was to transport secret materials from ship to shore and back, during which missions he carried a .45 pistol. When the *Shipley Bay* gave support in battle, communications officer Millar received the radio messages regarding daily changes in battle lines and communicated those to the pilots of the planes served by the carrier.

Millar's own writing was done in cramped and often noisy quarters, in tropical heat that (as the ship shuttled back and forth from Hawaii to Guam) was often sweltering. With the heat at its worst, the ship's walls were painful to touch; and ink wouldn't dry.

Sometimes Millar used an upturned wastebasket as a stool when he wrote in his improvised workspace. When his eight-man room became too boisterous, he asked for transfer back to a two-man compartment below the waterline, in "Torpedo Junction," beneath where the planes were stored.

Millar often felt alienated, politically and culturally, from his shipmates ("The word is inarticulate"); he craved a sort of intellectual stimulation that probably couldn't be found outside the academy. But if there were no other intellectuals on the *Shipley Bay*, there were several cheerful people able and willing to give Millar practical aid. The captain, a member of the Detective Book Club, loaned him mysteries. A warrant officer with access to legal-toxicology texts provided technical info on poisons which Millar hoped to use in *The Long Ride*. A Navy public relations man (probably in Honolulu) bought Millar a beer and gave official clearance for his thriller's plot; the p.r. man was a former editorial assistant at the *American* magazine — and a fellow client of Kenneth and Margaret Millar's New York agent Harold Ober.

By mid-April, Ken Millar was properly launched on his *Ride*, and he told his wife: "I think I'm writing freer dialogue than I did in *Tunnel* ... I think it's going to be OK."

Margaret had great news of her own to relate in April:

she'd bought them a house in Santa Barbara, California — a town she said was nearly as beautiful as La Jolla. Enthusiastically she wrote Ken with details of their new home, its lovely city, and the acquaintances she'd already made, including a divorcee who was "not my soul-mate, but she does have a car, a fair am't of dough & a rather lively manner. (She also hunts wild pigs in the mountains at night with her boy friend, a detective here)."

Millar declared himself thrilled with this development: "I never dreamed I could have such nostalgia for a place I have never seen. But Santa Barbara is my spiritual home ..." The town was his "Ithaca at the moment," he announced, "because my Penelope is there weaving her web of words." And he said: "Your friend (and her detective! did you say detective?) sounds interesting."

Margaret had even more amazing California news in June: Warner Bros. had bought film rights to *The Iron Gates* for $15,000 and was hiring her to write its script for $750 a week! Millar shared in the euphoria when he got word of his wife's spectacular good fortune on June 22: "My shipmates tell me I've been looking very well indeed the last few hours." He was full of encouragement for Margaret, and couldn't help observing "Hemingway got only 12 grand" from Warners for his book *To Have and Have Not*.

Around the same time as this remarkable development, Millar's ship took part in its only combat of World War Two. "Okinawa became ours yesterday," Ensign Millar wrote Margaret on June 22. Soon the *Shipley Bay* was headed Stateside.

No city had ever looked better to Ken Millar than the San Francisco he saw come into view in late July. If his earlier arrival in southern California had been psychologically meaningful, how much more must it have meant for him now to catch sight of this northern California port, his virtual birthplace.

Ensign Millar was reunited with his wife in San Francisco, after five months' separation. The couple enjoyed a week's leave together (Margaret had arranged for Linda's former nursery-school teacher from Michigan to look after the Millars' six-year-old in Santa Barbara) before parting on the very eve of Maggie's taking the train to southern California and the Warners lot.

When Margaret arrived at Warner Bros., it was love at first sight. The writers' building was full of famous authors. Maggie had an office down the hall from William Faulkner. Frequent *New Yorker* contributor John Collier drove her home (to the Hollywood Roosevelt Hotel) after her first day. Others on hire at the studio this season included W.R. Burnett (*Little Caesar*, *High Sierra*), the young Englishman Christopher Isherwood, Kurt Siodmak (*Donovan's Brain*) and Elliot Paul (*The Last Time I Saw Paris*, *Hugger-Mugger in the Louvre*). One of Margaret's first duties was to view Warners' 1941 version of Dashiell Hammett's *The Maltese Falcon*, starring Humphrey Bogart as private detective Sam Spade, to see how closely movie followed book ("Pretty good picture," Maggie reported, "Bogart's damn good"). A few days later, she saw the studio's as-yet unreleased version of Raymond Chandler's *The Big Sleep*, this time with Bogart as private eye Philip Marlowe. These were heady days.

When the *Shipley Bay* put in to San Diego for several weeks' repairs, Ken Millar saw Warners for himself, on August 14, 1945. It proved a memorable visit. That afternoon, Japan's surrender became official: World War Two was over. The Millars celebrated by having dinner and many drinks with Elliot Paul and his wife, after which Maggie and Paul had a two-hour marathon playing session at the two pianos in the Pauls' Hollywood living room.

Ken Millar's L.A. leave was memorable also for an encounter with William Faulkner, who spoke with the Millars about a range of things: from Herman Melville to his daughter's mare about to foal down in Oxford, Mississippi. "We ... found," Millar wrote later, "that the fieriest imagination of our time resides in the gentlest of men." Only weeks earlier, Millar had been reading much Faulkner aboard ship and writing Maggie in wonder about "the unholy grandeur" of "maybe the best novelist" America had. A year from now, Ken, speaking for himself and Margaret, would claim Faulkner as "the favorite author of both of us." Millar the literary scholar read Faulkner (one of three writers given credit for the script of *The Big Sleep*) as, among other things, a mystery novelist; he called Faulkner's book *Sanctuary* "about the best detective story I've read." He asked Margaret about a *Sanctuary* plot subtlety: "Did you get the impression that Temple's father framed (Popeye) for the murder he was hanged for? That isn't explained." (This Faulknerian ambiguity might be the inspiration for a recurring element in later Macdonald books: a final fact uncovered but uncommented on by the detective, though left in plain view for readers to perceive.) After shaking hands with Faulkner, Ken Millar joked he'd never wash his hand again.

Warners visits aside, Millar spent most of his three-week leave at the Chapman Park Hotel (where Margaret had moved from the Roosevelt), "writing laboriously and unenthusiastically on my still-to-be-stillborn thriller," as he reported to their Michigan mystery-writer friend H.C. Branson, "while Margaret went to the office to earn unimaginable sums ..." Millar was sincerely pleased with his wife's success, but he was keenly aware of the new disparity between their salaries. The earnings gap made him uneasy, as did the great professional distance his wife had put between them. Millar needed some way to catch up, however modestly.

One possibility presenting itself was to enter a short story contest being sponsored this year by *Ellery Queen's Mystery Magazine*, a competition soliciting entries from the country's top detective and crime writers (including William Faulkner).

Launched in 1941 (the one-hundredth anniversary of the first mystery story, Poe's "The Murders in the Rue Morgue") by Frederic Dannay, who with his cousin Manfred B. Lee had written popular detective fiction since 1929 as Ellery Queen, the digest-sized *EQMM* had done much to revive and sustain the mystery short story. Now Queen was doing even more, with a competition offering thousands of dollars in prize money. Both Millars talked of entering the well-publicized contest.

The challenge was on Ken Millar's mind the last days of his leave, as he and Margaret returned with their daughter and her nanny to Santa Barbara and Ken saw for the first time the home his wife had made for them at 2124 Bath. (He'd work the house and its address into a scene in *The Long Ride*.) When leave ended, he returned to San Diego for two weeks (accompanied by his family), then shipped out on September 26.

The *Shipley Bay* had been converted to a troop transport, to pick up servicemen from posts far and near and ferry them back to the States. On Millar's second night aboard, his fertile subconscious concocted a surreal mystery plot which he sardonically described to Margaret: "I dreamed a queer dream: a complete murder story, or so it seemed, with suspects, atmosphere, detection, and surprises. The corpse was a woman at first and towards the end a man, all without explanation. Also without explanation, it was the corpse who turned out to be the murderer. So it looks as if I won't be able to use the plot for the Ellery Queen contest, unless their standards become surprisingly elastic."

If his dream wouldn't do for *Ellery Queen's Mystery Magazine*, it would certainly have intrigued Karen Horney, the psychoanalyst whose book Millar was reading and liking this week (and which may have fed his fertile subconscious). "Reading a book like that," Millar wrote his wife, "is seeing myself in practically every case-history ... every neurotic type ... *You*, of course, are the other person I'm always looking for ..." He didn't think either of them were actual neurotics, Millar assured Margaret. "Still, I intend to be analyzed after the war ... I'm interested and should learn from the experience, I hope not too much." In the meantime, Millar told Margaret, "I don't after all have a copy of [the *EQMM*] contest-rules and I'm still interested, so if you have 'em send 'em along or better bring them to Frisco ..."

Margaret did that when she met Millar again in San Francisco on October 9 for four days. Neither of them had yet decided to enter the Ellery Queen contest; but the final night of Millar's stay, Kenneth and Margaret met someone who persuaded them they should: William A.P. White, a writer best known by his pen name of Anthony Boucher.

The 34-year-old Boucher, equally involved with mystery fiction and science fiction, wore many hats: novelist, short-story writer, translator (notably, later, of Jorge Luis Borges's first tale published in English), eventual magazine and book editor, radio scriptwriter (*The New Adventures of Sherlock Holmes*, *The Adventures of Ellery Queen*, though the latter was a well-kept secret), and — most importantly for the Millars — critic. Boucher covered crime fiction in the *San Francisco Chronicle*; in a few years, he'd become mystery reviewer for the *New York Times*. A charter member of the newly-formed Mystery Writers of America, Anthony Boucher was well on his way to being the most influential detective-fiction critic in the country; and he was a fan of both Margaret and Kenneth Millar's work.

Boucher, who lived in Berkeley, came to the Millars' hotel on a Thursday night to share several rounds of cocktails. The critic had given Margaret's *The Iron Gates* what Ken thought its best-written and smartest review, in the *Chronicle*; now he congratulated Kenneth Millar on *The Dark Tunnel*, a mention of which he'd work into his essay on spy fiction for Howard Haycraft's 1946 anthology *The Art of the Mystery Story*. It wasn't fair, Boucher joked, that so much writing talent should exist in one family. He strongly encouraged the Millars to submit entries in the Ellery Queen contest. (He also urged they join the Mystery Writers of America, which they would.)

"I liked Boucher ...," Millar wrote Margaret a few days later from sea, "a good guy, and intelligent enough for keeps." (Margaret liked him too, but she said: "Sorry I got plastered Thurs. p.m. No wonder. Next time we see Boucher let's start Later.")

"Anthony Boucher's few words of praise and the inspiration of you had such a bracing effect on me that Friday night (the day we left ...)," Millar told his wife, "I sat down and wrote 10 pages on a story, which I know isn't good enough for the EQMM but still it's writing ... 'Low Tide Murder' the title — I worked it all out Friday night. It's good only sporadically, I know, but the good parts are what interest me."

In this short story (which he'd retitle "Death by Air"), he announced to Margaret, he was developing a detective who'd be a "successor" to Chandler's Philip Marlowe, and a style "which I'll go on with for a bit till I hit pay dirt."

The character, who would indeed lead Millar to pay dirt, came to life aboard the *Shipley Bay*; but he'd been conceived, in a manner of speaking, in a San Francisco hotel room — not far from where Millar himself had been born some thirty years before.

### ✗ ✗ ✗

Within the clan, as in other branches of literature, there has developed a sharp split between the advocates of realism and the champions of a less violent picture of life. Raymond Chandler (who was given the doubtful distinction in one pulp magazine of being "the best blood-and-sex writer to come up since Dashiell Hammett") dedicated his *Five Murderers* to a former pulp editor, Joseph Thompson Shaw, "in memory of the time when we were trying to get murder away from the upper classes, the week-end house party and the vicar's rose garden, and back to the people who are really good at it." This dedication bears for the admirer of the rough-and-tough detective story the same ringing challenge that Wordsworth's famous preface to the *Lyrical Ballads* contained for the Romantic poets.

Richard C. Boys, "The Detective Story Today," *The Quarterly Review of the Michigan Alumnus*, Spring 1945

Millar's detective was a Santa Barbara private eye named Rogers, who spoke in a Chandleresque cadence: "My initial fee is one hundred dollars. After that I charge people according to how much I think I can get out of them." Some of the people Rogers met had the same last names as a few of Millar's shipmates; and Rogers' client seemed obliquely inspired by a recurring character from Anthony Boucher's fiction.

Millar had pointedly sought out Boucher's work as soon as he got back to the *Shipley Bay*; the captain loaned him one novel Boucher had had an anonymous hand in rewriting. If Millar read any of Boucher's four books about L.A. p.i. Fergus O'Breen, he'd have encountered that eye's sister Maureen O'Breen, "head of publicity at Metropolis Pictures." Millar's Rogers is hired in "Death by Air" by one Millicent Dreen, who does "national publicity for Tele-Pictures."

On October 17, Millar told Margaret he was "nearly finished my story (wrote 14 pages last night, was up practically all night) of which I am not proud but I'm proud of myself for getting down to writing again. I'll write more stories and eventually get pretty good — I hope — then I'll go on with my book. It's wonderful what a little practice will do for one's expression. Also, when I really get into it, I love writing."

Doing this Rogers opus was prompting notions for other possible contest entries, Millar said — for instance, "a story which I'm almost afraid to write it's going to be so terrible: about the crime, flight, and hunting down of a sex maniac — entitled *The Tribulations of Mr. Small*. I'll write it, by gum, even if I am afraid to, as soon as we get out of Pearl ... This contest, you see is for both *crime* and detective stories. Altogether, I have ideas for about six stories, one or two of which would make books. But the important thing, isn't it, is to get some writing done, get into the groove, *feel* like a writer (so difficult for me still," Millar reminded his prolific book-writing wife, "since I lack your wonderful assurance.)"

Soon he could say of his Rogers tale: "Finished my story, between 9-10,000 words. Wish it were better ..."

It was good enough. Though a bit awkward, this first-person story had energy and style. It was clearly inspired by Chandler, and its downbeat ending recalled Dashiell Hammett; but its delight in language, its droll one-liners, its ironic tone, and its fast pace seemed fresh and all Millar's own. The story flashed intriguing glimpses of Hollywood types at work and at play (drawn with the authority of Millar's visits to his wife's new world) and candid snaps of a southern California already in transition from wartime to postwar. With its foreshadowings and elaborate similes, the story was something out of the ordinary, and also a highly professional piece of prose: in some ways not as good as Chandler, but in others maybe half a step ahead. Its few pages covered a lot of ground: Santa Barbara beach cottage, Wilshire Boulevard apartment, San Fernando Valley ranch house, Hollywood movie lot, Sunset Strip night club, coroner's office. In its geographical range, it prefigured the long, book-length odysseys of Lew Archer, the first of which was three years in the future. Also presaging things to come in the Archer books were this tale's intergenerational betrayals and jealousies, and its diseased moral climate, in which evil is contagious and guilt shared. Ken Millar sowed the seeds for a thirty-year career as a detective novelist in one quickly-written short story.

Millar left these pages onboard ship when he met again with Margaret for a few days in late October in San Francisco, at the Fairmont. The couple's parting came all too soon; in the rush, Millar left his navy-blue raincoat at the hotel. Back on ship, a lonely Millar wrote his wife: "I drowned my sorrows in reading."

This year saw republication of many works by an American author Ken Millar first read as a teenager in Ontario, Canada: F. Scott Fitzgerald. This was the writer in whose books Millar now submerged himself, in weeks during which he wrote and rewrote pages that would make a prototype for his eventual life's-work. Later Millar would say he'd learned more about style and technique from Fitzgerald than from any other writer. Some fruits of those lessons may even be seen in his very earliest private-eye stories.

*Tender Is the Night* was the first Fitzgerald book Ken Millar read on the *Shipley Bay*. He consumed it in one evening, finding it "marvellous. In writing and conception of human relations and depth of tragic perception, it's easily his best book ... Nicole, with her 'white crooks' eyes,' is an amazing creation ..." For contrast, Millar next read most of

James T. Farrell's *Studs Lonigan*: "pretty powerful, with a terrific ending — but oh so depressing" — so much so, he put it aside and went back to his own fiction.

Millar began penning a second case for private eye Rogers, who now acquired the first name Joe. "Death by Water" began at a southern California bungalow hotel, the Valeria Pueblo, which closely resembled places the Millars had recently stayed, including the Casa Mañana in La Jolla and the Chapman Park in L.A.

"I wrote 14 pages on my second detective story and re-wrote the first," Millar reported to Margaret on November 2. "Neither, I'm afraid, is good enough for Ellery Queen — I just don't seem to be able to *put out* in a short detective story." But the tales were serving a useful purpose: "getting me back in the writing groove — the words are coming easier again ... I'll probably write a third story just for the hell of it ..."

He told his wife, "Like you, I have a hard time thinking in the short story form: I either get really interested in my characters or can't get interested at all ... My writing time is too short these days to lavish loving care on a couple of half-assed mystery shorts ..." But he asked Margaret: "Can you check for me whether a murderer can inherit money from his victim in California?"

On November 4, he announced, "I just mailed to you registered first class the first two cases of Joe Rogers whoever he may be, Death by Air (nearly 10,000) and Death by Water (over 7,000)." Neither, he repeated, was good enough; and only one could be published, he felt, since the murder-methods were too similar. Yet: "it feels good to have written them and I really *enjoyed* writing for the first time in ages ... If either or both of the stories looks at all hopeful to you, please edit them or it as drastically as possible, have 'em typed and send 'em off through [Ober agent] Ivan [von Auw] to arrive by December 3 ... I know they need rewriting (I wrote the final 15 pages of *Water* straight away in one sitting today) but I haven't the time or inclination ..."

He did find time for more of his new favorite writer. "The more I read of Fitzgerald, the crazier I am about him," Millar told Margaret, "especially his style — high, chaste, romantic and colloquial at once, the very essence of the ideal style and thus of course lacking a little weight and warmth — and his ability to put a bloom, a priceless loving quality, on people and their relations. His main defect is an idealizing tendency, which makes his characters a little too good to be true even when they're bad ... Still, what a writer, and how much he has to teach about writing (he understood style and technique both generally and in detail better than any other U.S. writer ...). It practically makes me weep to read those waltzing paragraphs: what an eye and ear and touch." Millar's re-immersion in Fitzgerald, at the age of nearly-thirty, and his first-ever reading of *Tender Is the Night*, seemed to have as profound an effect on him as had reading Dickens at ten, Hammett at fifteen, and Chandler at twenty-five. After writing the above to Margaret, Millar sat down the same night and re-read *The Great Gatsby* straight through: something he'd later do almost yearly. Then he read all the Fitzgerald short stories he could find, and asked Margaret to send him *The Crack-Up*.

Beside such grace, his own efforts seemed puny. Millar was self-deprecating about his recent private-eye tales: "I seriously doubt that I'll ever set the Sacramento River on fire with my mystery shorts, don't you?" But at the same time, he said, "I feel quite smugly happy about getting back to writing and liking it." And he was fond of the characters he'd created, "Air" 's Millicent Dreen and "Water" 's the Ralstons, "though both are limned with unnecessary crudity ..." In fact, he thought, "*Water could* make a nice crappy little mystery novel, maybe, huh?"

Millar asked that Maggie add a tag line to "Water" if she found out about the inheritance aspect: "Either: It worked, John'll get it. Or: The irony of it the effort was wasted, John won't get the money anyway on account of – (I think the latter is correct but wouldn't know.)" After consulting a toxicology text, Millar sent his wife some rewritten lines to insert into a coroner's explanation of a drowning in "Death by Air."

Margaret pronounced herself thrilled with the Rogers stories: "Was utterly delighted at your dialogue & the *freer flow* of things. There's *nothing* amateur in them." She wrote a final paragraph for "Water" as instructed, made the inserts he'd requested, had the stories professionally typed and sent them to New York for submission.

Margaret too was working on a story for the contest; hearing it described, her husband said, "It sounds like the sort of thing that could cop a prize by originality and good writing ..."

Stimulated by his Rogers efforts, Millar found he now had "plenty of good ideas for shorts — too many — but would hate to spend too much time unprofitably." Still he took time to write a third competition entry — not "The Tribulations of Mr. Small" but a grim murder story titled "Shock" (told completely in dialogue, and finished in four hours) which he mailed from the south Pacific directly to Ellery Queen.

With his *EQMM* "duties" out of the way, Millar returned to his novel. He was able to brag to Margaret in mid-November: "I am proud to report that I've added, in the last four days, 8000 words to *Ride* — not all of it good, by any means, but all of it wordage, and some of it good, in varying ways ... Ain't it hard, though, to handle a bunch of people on a train trip? ... I've fluffed it quite badly but I don't give a damn ... [W]hat I want is to finish this book, my personal albatross, and never think of it again."

# Introduction

As he wrote, the *Shipley Bay* made its way to the atoll of Kwajalein and back. In addition to writing, as usual Millar read: Don Marquis' *Archy and Mehitabel*, Ann Arbor friend Henry Branson's latest mystery *The Fearful Passage* ("quietly perfect ... damn good"); and *Prater Violet*, a brief novel about a film producer, by one of Maggie's Warners co-workers, Chris Isherwood. "As a piece of technical work," Millar said of the latter, "the book can teach me plenty: it has an easy grace and deceptive casualness that I find very enviable." But not as enviable as the traits of his latest literary hero: "A page of the letters Fitzgerald dashed off almost invariably has more meat than one of Isherwood's very carefully written pages," Millar maintained. "Compared with Fitzgerald, Isherwood doesn't seem very much alive." He went back to re-reading Margaret's gift copy to him of Fitzgerald's *The Crack-Up*.

Millar the writer continued to make good progress on *The Long Ride*. When he learned late in December he'd be discharged from the service next March 15, he wondered if that might not give him just "time enough ... to run another book through the mill."

Meanwhile the current one needed last-minute research. Two days before Christmas, Millar finally managed to reach a Honolulu detective by telephone from the Navy Yard to verify Hawaiian police procedure and terminology for his book's early scenes. *The Suicides* (his new title for *The Long Ride*) was ready to be typed. A shipmate prepared the manuscript for Millar, so sick of typewriters after his *Shipley Bay* duty he wouldn't touch one for the rest of his life. The author fed *Suicides* to his buddy one chapter at a time, "so the suspense will be an incentive to go on typing in the heat."

"Having written hard and daily" for two months, Millar gave himself the holiday "to see what pops up in my mind to write next." He wanted to turn "Death by Water" into a book but couldn't make plans until hearing whether Ellery Queen had bought the short story ("doubtful, but a possibility"). One non-detective novel he considered writing was a "rustic story" based on an Ontario family whose farm he'd worked on before college: "You may sneer," he wrote Maggie, "but if I could do it right it'd be a best-seller."

While mulling his next literary move, Millar "buried" himself "(shallowly) in inconsequential reading," including the non-fiction *Viking Murder Book* anthology; and viewed "some of the more unlovely examples of American movie making," including *Fog Island* — "in which one guy is followed by another guy who is followed by another guy who is followed by another guy. You think I'm exaggerating? You're an optimist." Other shipboard movies in December included *Fired Wife* ("continuously embarrassing"), *She Gets Her Man* ("just moderately terrible"), *Boom Town*, *White Cargo*, and *Iceland*, with Sonja Henie doing the hula ("*really* embarrassing"). Of the *Shipley Bay* cinema, Millar cracked: "You pays no money and you gets no choice."

He also read a text Maggie had given him on how to write "Fast Detective stories" for Clayton Rawson, an editor at *True Detective* and *Master Detective* magazines, which he thought (as she did) good: "while it didn't encourage me to write Fast (D.) stories — I prefer fiction what is fiction – I ... was stimulated to sit right down and do a complete outline for another spy book ... a 24-hour job, fast and mysterious with romance in it even." "The Box" would take place in San Francisco, he said, or maybe Panama; and Millar hoped to submit it when written to the *Saturday Evening Post*. "Nope, I've got no delusions of grandeur," he assured his wife, "... I'm just going to have a try is all."

Ken Millar was anxious to make his way as a professional writer; he'd allow himself one postwar year to see if he could earn a living by his pen alone. He aspired to be an outstanding mainstream-fiction writer and felt he had the requisite talent (upon reading a book of John Steinbeck short stories, he told Margaret: "I could do as well, I believe"), but — despite his wife's urging him otherwise — he intended to establish himself at first through crime fiction: a genre which, from his point of view, need not be inferior, encompassing (as he felt) such authors as Dickens, Greene, and Faulkner. (In 1946, he'd tell Ellery Queen: "I consider Hemingway's 'Short Happy Life of F. Macomber' probably the best murder story in the language …' ")

(Even as Margaret was urging her gifted husband to write mainstream fiction instead, Millar was telling his capable wife she made a mistake by limiting herself to suspense: "What nonsensical compulsion makes you suppose you must always write mysteries, when you can outwrite, outthink, and out-observe nine-tenths of the bestselling *straight* novelists now writing? … Why your absurd humility towards the novel form, which is exploited so successfully by your inferiors?")

Kenneth Millar's mystery-writing career (and no doubt his confidence) got a big boost in January 1946 when he received word from Margaret that one of his stories (which one, not yet known) had won a $300 Fourth Prize in the Ellery Queen contest. Millar guessed (correctly) it was "Death by Air." "The chief reason I'm so pleased," he wrote his wife, "… is that it makes it so certain that I'll be able to turn pro without any strain." He was also happy to note: "Dannay is bringing out all the prize winners in a book (good publicity for me … among detective fans!)" Millar consoled his wife on her own entry's failure to snag a prize: "You needn't feel badly about your story — as I said it was much too good for that market." (William Faulkner's *EQMM* submission took second-place honors.)

In the wake of his prize-winning entrance into the mystery-writing community, Millar chose next to read S.S. Van Dine's bestselling 1927 detective novel *The "Canary"*

*Murder Case*, featuring sleuth Philo Vance. "Not a bad puzzle," Millar allowed in a letter to Margaret, "but the writing doesn't pass muster. Dreadfully pretentious, to cover up lack of knowledge about people and their feelings. Deadly slow and insufferably snobbish. Not as good as [Margaret's 1941 debut book *The Invisible Worm*], I think. Yet it's gone through 20 or so editions. There's one field where it paid off to be a pioneer. One similarity to Raymond Chandler: the masses of detail, which fill up most of the wordage. But unlike Raymond, there isn't enough action, drama, or character to make a good novelette. And if you think I can't write dialogue, try some more Dine. He writes the way I talk when I'm trying to be funny in a queer academic way. French and Italian phrases average one or two a page, and one of them at least is a hideous boner." (Later in this letter, after some highflown sentences about public and private virtue, Millar exclaimed: "Gracious, I'm getting *serieux, ma cherie,* as *Philo* Vance would *dicere, n-est-ce pas?*") Reader Millar abandoned Van Dine for a book by psychologist William James.

The almost cruise-ship calm of the *Shipley Bay* in the waning weeks of now-Lt. j.g. Kenneth Millar's postwar Naval service was broken the evening of January 18, 1946, by the Shipley Bay's participation in a rescue at sea of the thirteen-man crew of a downed flying boat. "It was a perfect night for a rescue," Millar reported to Margaret. "Bright full moon. Fairly calm sea." Mission safely accomplished, Millar sat down and for about ninety minutes made notes of some of his plot notions. "It appears that I have ideas for 20 books!" he informed his wife. "Maybe 10 of them are worth writing. Maybe 5 of them will be written (because by that time I'll have ideas for others ...) Anyway, my postwar plan includes plenty of work ..."

Again he wished he knew which of his stories Ellery Queen had bought: "It would give me something to go on with, since

I'd like to write them another story or two (I have a couple of ideas — plenty, in fact, since any 'tec. novel can be written as a short story.)" In the next days he plotted two mystery shorts but refrained from writing them in his cramped shipboard quarters, in the tropical heat: "I don't want to force too much production under difficult conditions, for fear that it will destroy my enthusiasm for writing, my élan, my passion in a word. I don't want to become (or continue as) a hack ..."

By February, Millar had at last learned which Joe Rogers story Ellery Queen had bought: as he'd suspected, it was "Death by Air," though the magazine gave it a new name. On February 12, Millar informed Anthony Boucher by letter of "a hard-boiled short (re-titled *Find the Woman)* which got me fourth prize and three C's (as they say in hard-boiled stories). I can say with certainty that I'd never have written it if you hadn't urged me to, so this is on the lines of a 'but for whom.' "

He also wouldn't have written it if Ellery Queen hadn't founded a magazine and given a contest. But whatever professional gratitude Ken Millar felt towards Ellery Queen, he didn't let it cloud the critical eye with which he read their fiction — a critical eye he needed to keep in sharp focus if he hoped to reach the artistic summit of his newly-chosen field. "Brought up [Queen's 1942 book] *Calamity Town* to read on watch," Millar wrote his wife in mid-February, "but boggled a bit after 2 pages ... What a difference style makes. If a book hasn't got it I can read it only with difficulty, and EQ ain't got it, though how they try ..."

✗ ✗ ✗

... only one of the fifteen prizewinners in EQMM's first contest is classifiable as a hardboiled detective story. Even that one — Kenneth Millar's "Find the Woman" — is not a pure hardboiler. True, it presents in Rogers, the private dick, a Hammett-Chandler tough hombre; it offers a hard, realistic crime situation ...  And yet with all this, Kenneth Millar's story is not pure hardboiledism: its characters are not psychologically black-and-white, and there are undertones and over-tones in "Find the Woman" not usually woven into the fabric of tough 'tecs. ... Kenneth Millar's first book was *The Dark Tunnel* (Dodd, Mead), an excellent novel of suspense and pursuit in which the author "tried to treat a romantic and melodramatic plot in a realistic manner, with a hero who is not particularly heroic ..." Those are Mr. Millar's own words and we wonder if they don't describe his short story, "Find the Woman," much more accurately and pointedly than your Editor has ...

Ellery Queen, *Ellery Queen's Mystery Magazine*, June 1946

Discharged from active duty in the spring of 1946, Ken Millar joined his wife and child in Santa Barbara, where he felt the urgent need to get a few books under his professional belt.  His mostly-shipboard-written thriller *The Suicides* was bought by Dodd, Mead, to be published as *Trouble Follows Me*.  (To the author's dismay, Dodd, Mead rejected *The Suicides* title as "not box-office.")  Millar quickly wrote two more crime novels, *Blue City* and *The Three Roads*, which his agent sold to the much more prestigious publishing house of Alfred A. Knopf.

Millar also did some half a dozen mainstream short stories after the war — only one of which, after six months' submissions, was bought for publication.  The pragmatic Millar learned a lesson: in future, he wouldn't spend time on short stories unless a viable market presented itself.

One did in 1948.  Ivan von Auw at the Harold Ober Agency suggested Millar try writing a story for the *American*, a slick magazine with a predominantly female readership.  Millar had met one of the *American*'s former editorial workers in the Navy: the public relations man who'd cleared the plot of *Trouble Follows Me*. He'd told Millar what that glossy's "very successful editorial policy" was: "promising the readers sex (e.g. through illustrations) but not giving it to them. It always works — see also the movies ..."

Yet the *American* regularly printed good mystery stories, and von Auw thought he could sell them something by Ken. Millar gave it a try. The result was "The Bearded Lady," a novelette narrated by Sam Drake, the lead character from *Trouble Follows Me*. When it was bought, Millar was as discouraged as he was grateful. If he could so easily meet the *American*'s calculating standards, maybe he was in real danger of becoming a hack.

Between *The Three Roads* and "The Bearded Lady," Millar wrote a novel-length work of mainstream fiction, *Winter Solstice*, which he judged unsuccessful and shelved without showing to a publisher. His next attempted book was *The Snatch*, a private-eye novel whose protagonist, Lew Archer, was essentially the same character as Joe Rogers, the southern California detective in the pair of *Shipley Bay* short stories written three years earlier.

Alfred Knopf balked at accepting *The Snatch*, claiming it inferior to the two Kenneth Millar novels his firm had printed. But when Millar instructed his agent to submit the manuscript elsewhere under the pseudonym "John Macdonald," Knopf reversed himself and published this "Macdonald" book in 1949 as *The Moving Target*.

A complaint by another writer, John D. MacDonald, caused Millar to change his new pseudonym to "John Ross Macdonald" for his next six books, including the second Lew Archer novel: 1950's *The Drowning Pool*. (Not until 1956 would he be known simply as "Ross Macdonald.")

Macdonald's first books earned strongly positive reviews

from mystery-fiction critics (notably Anthony Boucher). Lew Archer was well-launched as a series character by 1950, year of the sixth annual *Ellery Queen's Mystery Magazine* short-story contest. Millar/Macdonald wrote a long entry for this competition, "Strangers in Town" — the first Lew Archer short story *per se*. But (as with "Death by Water"), he soon saw the story's possibilities as a novel; he had it withdrawn from submission. "Strangers in Town" would provide the skeleton for the fourth Lew Archer novel, *The Ivory Grin* (written in 1951, published in 1952). (Millar also used elements of "Strangers in Town" in his 1953 story "The Imaginary Blonde," collected as "Gone Girl.")

Ken Millar next wrote short crime fiction for *Manhunt*, a digest-sized magazine that debuted in January 1953. No women's-magazine sensibility to worry about here; *Manhunt* aspired to revive the hard-boiled tradition of classic pulps such as *Black Mask*, while riding the coattails of Mickey Spillane's phenomenal popularity. Spillane was in the first issue of *Manhunt* — as was Kenneth Millar, with "Shock Treatment": that third story written (in four hours) aboard ship for the 1945 *EQMM* contest.

Macdonald published four new Lew Archer novelettes in *Manhunt* in the next twelve months. The rates were good, and the editors were eager.

And in 1953 he also wrote an Archer story for that year's Ellery Queen contest. Margaret Millar entered the *EQMM* event too — her first "official" try at the competition, since her 1945 entry was never publicly acknowledged. John Ross Macdonald's "Wild Goose Chase" won a third prize in this ninth annual *EQMM* event — while Margaret Millar's "The Couple Next Door" won a second prize.

In 1954, all Macdonald's published private-eye stories were gathered between soft covers by his paperback house, Bantam Books. "I thought up that thing and got it going," editor Saul

David recalled. "I was always looking for ways with pet writers — and he was one of the people I really liked a lot — to get them extra money. One of the ways was to do anthologies, 'cause they had all written short stories — novellas and things. The audience never really loved that kind of thing — they wanted novels by and large — but if the writer was popular enough, you could in effect get away with it."

Joe Rogers and Sam Drake both became Lew Archer for this collection, which could then legitimately be titled *The Name Is Archer*. Millar rewrote all seven stories at least slightly. He took the romantic bits out of "The Bearded Lady" and put in a fist fight. In the *Manhunt* novelettes, he removed some of the more violent details.

*The Name Is Archer* was a surprise hit — a surprise to Millar, anyway — and maybe that caused its author to take ballpoint in hand and do another Archer novelette, "The Angry Man." This time apparently the story's potential as a novel was so obvious Millar didn't bother to have his handwritten pages typed. "The Angry Man" stayed in one of his spiral-bound plot notebooks for future reference. In time it became the basis of the 1958 Archer novel *The Doomsters*.

Once that novel was written (but before it was published), the story underwent still more permutations. Having sold two previous books to *Cosmopolitan* magazine for condensation, Millar did an abridged version of *The Doomsters* on spec for Cosmo. When it was rejected (partly because the magazine's editors found the idea of a female killer distasteful), Millar rewrote his abridgment, changing the villain to a male. This draft was also turned down by Cosmo; it sold, though, to *EQMM*, where eventually it was printed in 1962 as "Bring the Killer to Justice."

✗ ✗ ✗

A new crime-fiction journal launched in 1960 prompted the writing of the penultimate Lew Archer short story.

The digest was *Ed McBain's Mystery Magazine*. Millar was in the middle of writing the ninth Lew Archer novel, *The Wycherly Woman*, when this publication asked for an Archer novelette.

"I was sorta conned into it, in a way," Millar remembered later to journalist Paul Nelson. "An editor wanted me to do it, and I said I wouldn't but that I would give it thought or something. He came back saying, my name was on the cover and I *had* to write it. You know, it's an old trick ... That's what got the story written: I thought I *had* to."

The writer took five days off from his novel to pen a story, "Midnight Blue," then went right back to work on the book. "It's the sort of thing you shouldn't do," he told Nelson. "That isn't the way to produce good ones." But he conceded of "Midnight Blue": "Actually, it's not the *worst* of the stories."

The final Archer short story written and published, "The Sleeping Dog," was commissioned by a more unlikely periodical: *Sports Illustrated*.

In February 1964, a senior editor from that magazine contacted Millar and proposed Ross Macdonald do a 4,000- to 6,000-word Lew Archer story with a sports background of some sort. The editor, who was a great fan of Macdonald's work, said the sports hook could be slight. Millar was eager to try, though (again) he was in the middle of polishing a new book (*The Serpent's Tooth*, published as *The Far Side of the Dollar*), and very involved, as he told Ivan von Auw, as a Santa Barbara conservationist, "fighting a vocal public battle on behalf of the Calif. Condors, of which some sixty remain, and which are menaced by Forest Service policies."

He told the *Sports Illustrated* man about his fight to save the condors, too; and the editor had another idea: why didn't Macdonald write a quick nonfiction piece about that for *SI* as well?

Millar did, and the article ran in April. Once paid for the

article, Millar started work on the short story. "Having to include *sports* is rather a nuisance," he admitted to von Auw's partner Dorothy Olding, "but I think I'll lick it okay."

He met the requirement by hatching a plot that involved hunting and dog training. "The Sleeping Dog" was 6,000 words long and typically complex; Millar had to labor to keep the story down to *SI*'s limit. "It certainly contains the germ of a book," he thought. He mailed the story in August.

Alas, *Sports Illustrated* decided the short story's sporting peg was too thin after all, though they encouraged the author to try another one on them. Millar thought not. He made clear to Olding it hadn't been *his* fault: "[The editor's] original request to me, you should know, was quite vague, giving as one illustration of a 'sports background' 'sipping rum in the sun.' But I expected to have to waste a story to get from him the truth, which editors can constitutionally yield up only in the form of a negative reaction." He requested she sell the story elsewhere if she could.

"The Sleeping Dog" was submitted to and turned down by *The Saturday Evening Post*, *This Week*, and *Cosmopolitan* before *Argosy* bid $500. Millar said fine, and it was published there in April of '65.

Millar still thought the story had book or TV potential, but the experience of writing it "to order" and then having it rejected left a bad taste that lingered. When young publisher Otto Penzler contracted to collect all the Archer short stories in hardcover for the first time in 1976, Millar didn't want "The Sleeping Dog" included. (Penzler insisted it should be, and it was.)

✗ ✗ ✗

From first to last, Millar/Macdonald's short stories gave glimpses of (and opportunities for) Lew Archer's development as a character, and Ross Macdonald's growth as an artist – from the young but already skilled professional of 1945's

"Death by Air" and "Death by Water" to the older and wiser man of such 1960s masterworks as *The Chill*.

This mutual progress always held the keenest professional and personal interest for Kenneth Millar. As he told Charles Champlin of the *Los Angeles Times* in 1975, while working on what would prove to be the final Lew Archer novel: "Archer began as a child of the genre and gradually became an individual. I hope that that happened to his writer as well."

# NOTES

" 'books that poked their heads above the fog' ": Judge Lynch, "… let him die!" *Saturday Review*, January 6, 1945.

" 'Most of them were written in a hurry' ": Millar to John D. Sutcliffe, February 14, 1975; typed copy, the Kenneth Millar Papers, Special Collections and Archives UC Davis Libraries.

" 'I felt as if a very long, long circle had been completed' ": Millar interview with Arthur Kaye, UCI.

" 'The Pacific bears some resemblance' ": Kenneth Millar to Professor Louis I. Bredvold, March 10, 1945, Louis I. Bredvold Correspondence, Bentley Historical Library, University of Michigan.

" 'a work of almost insane penetration' ": Kenneth to Margaret Millar, February 25, 1945, K. Millar Papers, UCI.

" 'still a masterpiece' ": Ibid.

" 'no masterpiece' ": Ibid.

" 'often amusing' ": Kenneth to Margaret Millar, March 10, 1945, K Millar Papers, UCI.

" 'far and away' ": Kenneth to Margaret Millar, April 21, 1945, UCI. Millar had not read Oliver Onions before, but: "I remember my mother used to talk about him …"

" 'had a riproarious time' ": Kenneth to Margaret Millar, June 4, 1945, UCI; KM to MM, June 5, 1945, UCI.

" 'a stinker' ": Kenneth to Margaret Millar, March 5, 1945, UCI.

" 'the first really good movie' ": Kenneth to Margaret Millar, March 24,

1945, UCI.

" 'so bad'": Kenneth to Margaret Millar, March 12, 1945, UCI.

" 'really first class' ": Kenneth to Margaret Millar, March 4, 1945, UCI.

" 'playing around with ideas' ": Kenneth to Margaret Millar, March 14, 1945, UCI.

" 'the only place I imagine' ": Kenneth to Margaret Millar, March 12, 1945, UCI.

" 'psychological love-story' ": Kenneth to Margaret Millar, March 17, 1945, UCI.

" 'No doubt it doesn't mean much' ": Kenneth to Margaret Millar, March 22, 1945, UCI.

" 'the successor to *Tunnel*' ": Kenneth to Margaret Millar, March 23, 1945, UCI.

" 'I couldn't go to sleep' ": Kenneth to Margaret Millar, March 24, 1945, UCI.

" 'somewhat outlandish' ": Kenneth to Margaret Millar, March 28, 1945, UCI.

" 'treasured bits' ": Kenneth to Margaret Millar, March 30, 1945, UCI.

" 'In the light of what you've done' ": Kenneth to Margaret Millar, April 8, 1945, UCI.

" '[I]f Chandler ever brings out another' ": Kenneth to Margaret Millar, June 25, 1945, UCI.

" 'a stinker' ": Kenneth to Margaret Millar, April 2, 1945, UCI.

" 'a bum B picture' ": Kenneth to Margaret Millar, April 4, 1945, UCI.

" 'I lasted about 20 minutes' ": Kenneth to Margaret Millar, June 23,

1945, UCI.

" 'a prime stinker' ": Ibid.

" 'surely the world's most passive actress' ": Kenneth to Margaret Millar, June 5, 1945, UCI.

" 'started well' ": Kenneth to Margaret Millar, April 8, 1945, UCI.

" 'ghastly' ": Kenneth to Margaret Millar, May 29, 1945, UCI.

" 'at which I lasted ... just five minutes' ": Kenneth to Margaret Millar, April 4, 1945, UCI.
    Millar flattered himself and underestimated the movie-makers: the killer in this picture doesn't appear until much later.

" 'plays a fairly hot clarinet' ": Kenneth to Margaret Millar, June 7, 1945, UCI.

" ' "Don't Cry Baby" ' ": Kenneth to Margaret Millar, April 4, 1945, UCI.

"a song he urged amateur-pianist Maggie to put music to": Ibid.

" 'I'd not be averse' ": Kenneth to Margaret Millar, May 18, 1945, UCI.

" 'big slick material' ": Kenneth to Margaret Millar, April 4, 1945, UCI.

" 'The word is inarticulate' ": Kenneth to Margaret Millar, May 11, 1945, UCI.

" 'I think I'm writing freer' ": Kenneth to Margaret Millar, April 8, 1945, UCI.

" 'not my soul-mate' ": Margaret to Kenneth Millar, May 27, 1945, The Margaret Millar Papers, Special Collections and Archives, UC Irvine Libraries.

" 'I never dreamed' ": Kenneth to Margaret Millar, May 14, 1945, K. Millar Papers, UCI.

" 'Your friend (and her detective!)' ": Kenneth to Margaret Millar, June 5, 1945, UCI.

" 'My shipmates' ": Kenneth to Margaret Millar, June 22, 1945, UCI.

" 'Hemingway got only 12 grand' ": Kenneth to Margaret Millar, June 24, 1945, UCI.

" 'Okinawa' ": Kenneth to Margaret Millar, June 22, 1945, UCI.

"No city had ever looked better": Millar interview with Arthur Kaye, K. Millar Papers, UCI.

" 'Pretty good picture' ": Margaret to Kenneth Millar, July 28, 1945, M. Millar Papers, UCI.

" 'We ... found' ": Millar preface to "Find the Woman" in *Maiden Murders: Mystery Writers of America* (Harper, 1952).

" 'the unholy grandeur' ": Kenneth to Margaret Millar, June 12-13, 1945, M. Millar Papers, UCI.

" 'the favorite author' ": Millar to Fred Dannay, November 25, 1946, Frederic Dannay Papers, Rare Book and Manuscript Library, Columbia University.

" 'about the best detective story' ": Kenneth to Margaret Millar, December 17, 1945, K. Millar Papers, UCI.

" 'Did you get the impression' ": Ibid.

" 'writing laboriously' ": Millar to H. C. Branson, October 7, 1945, UCI.

" 'I dreamed a queer dream' ": Kenneth to Margaret Millar, September 28, 1945, UCI.

" 'Reading a book like that' ": Kenneth to Margaret Millar, September 30, 1945, UCI.

" 'I don't after all' ": Kenneth to Margaret Millar, September 28, 1945,

UCI.

" 'I liked Boucher' ": Kenneth to Margaret Millar, October 15, 1945, UCI.

" 'Sorry I got plastered' ": Margaret to Kenneth Millar, October 13, 1945, M. Millar Papers, UCI.

" 'Anthony Boucher's few words of praise' ": Kenneth to Margaret Millar, October 15, 1945, K. Millar Papers, UCI.

" 'My initial fee' ": Kenneth Millar, "Find the Woman," *Ellery Queen's Mystery Magazine*, June 1946; reprinted in *Maiden Murders*; reprinted in Macdonald, *The Name Is Archer* (Bantam Books, 1955), et al.

" 'nearly finished my story' ": Kenneth to Margaret Millar, October 17, 1945, UCI.

" 'a story which I'm almost afraid to write' ": Ibid.

"' Finished my story' ": Ibid.

" 'I drowned my sorrows' ": Kenneth to Margaret Millar, November 2, 1945, UCI.

" 'marvellous' ": Ibid.

" 'pretty powerful' ": Kenneth to Margaret Millar, November 3, 1945, UCI.

" 'I wrote 14 pages' ": Kenneth to Margaret Millar, November 2, 1945, UCI.

" 'Like you' ": Kenneth to Margaret Millar, November 3, 1945, UCI.

" 'I just mailed to you' ": Kenneth to Margaret Millar, November 4, 1945, UCI.

" 'The more I read of Fitzgerald' ": Kenneth to Margaret Millar, November 5, 1945, UCI.

" 'I seriously doubt' ": Kenneth to Margaret Millar, November 4, 1945,

UCI.

" 'I feel quite smugly happy' ": Ibid.

" 'Was utterly delighted' ": Margaret to Kenneth Millar, November 22, 1945, M. Millar Papers, UCI.

" 'It sounds like the sort of thing' ": Kenneth to Margaret Millar, November 4, 1945, K. Millar Papers, UCI.

" 'plenty of ideas' ": Kenneth to Margaret Millar, November 5, 1945, UCI.

" 'I am proud to report' ": Kenneth to Margaret Millar, November 11, 1945, UCI.

" 'quietly perfect' ": Kenneth to Margaret Millar, December 15, 1945, UCI.

" 'As a piece of technical work' ": Kenneth to Margaret Millar, December 1, 1945, UCI.

" 'time enough' ": Kenneth to Margaret Millar, December 20, 1945, UCI.

" 'so the suspense will be an incentive' ": Kenneth to Margaret Millar, December 30, 1945, UCI.

" 'Having written hard and daily' ": Kenneth to Margaret Millar, December 23, 1945, UCI.

" 'You may sneer' ": Kenneth to Margaret Millar, December 27, 1945, UCI.

" 'buried ... (shallowly)' ": Kenneth to Margaret Millar, December 28, 1945, UCI.

" 'some of the more unlovely examples' ": Ibid.

" 'You pays no money' ": Ibid.

" 'while it didn't encourage me' ": Kenneth to Margaret Millar, December 30, 1945, UCI.

" 'Nope, I've got no delusions of grandeur' ": Kenneth to Margaret Millar, January 4, 1946, UCI.

" 'I could do as well, I believe' ": Kenneth to Margaret Millar, January 2, 1946, UCI.

" 'I consider Hemingway's' ": Millar to Ellery Queen, November 14, 1946, Frederic Dannay Papers, Rare Book and Manuscript Library, Columbia University.

" 'You can't understand' ": Kenneth to Margaret Millar, December 20, 1945, K. Millar Papers, UCI.

" 'What nonsensical compulsion' ": Kenneth to Margaret Millar, December 1, 1945, UCI.

" 'The chief reason I'm so pleased' ": Kenneth to Margaret Millar, January 4, 1946, UCI.

" 'Not a bad puzzle' ": Kenneth to Margaret Millar, January 10, 1946, UCI.

" 'It was a perfect night' ": Kenneth to Margaret Millar, January 19, 1946, UCI.

" 'I don't want to force too much' ": Kenneth to Margaret Millar, January 20, 1946, UCI.

" 'a hard-boiled short' ": Millar to Wm. A.P. White (Anthony Boucher), February 12, 1946, courtesy Lilly Library, Indiana University.

" 'Brought up ... *Calamity Town*' ": Kenneth to Margaret Millar, February 15, 1946, K. Millar Papers, UCI.

" 'very successful editorial policy' ": Kenneth to Margaret Millar, April 1, 1945, UCI.

" 'I thought up that thing' ": Saul David interview with TN.

" 'I was sorta conned into it' ": Millar interview with Paul Nelson, K.

Millar Papers, UCI.

" 'fighting a vocal public battle' ": Millar to Ivan von Auw, February 20, 1964, Ober Archives, Manuscripts Division, Department of Rare Books and Special Collections, Princeton University Library.

" 'Having to include *sports*' ": Millar to Dorothy Olding, July 21, 1964, Ober Archives, Princeton.

" 'It certainly contains the germ of a book' ": Millar to Olding, August 7, 1964, Ober Archives, Princeton.

" '[The editor's] original request' ": Millar to Olding, August 21, 1964, Ober Archives, Princeton.

" 'Archer began as a child of the genre' ": Charles Champlin, *Los Angeles Times*, July 4, 1975.

# DEATH BY WATER

# DEATH BY WATER

## Preface by Tom Nolan

"I can think of few more complex critical enterprises," wrote Ross Macdonald, "than disentangling the mind and life of a first-person detective story writer from the mask of his detective-narrator."

In the case of Macdonald and his protagonist Lew Archer, the enterprise would prove especially rewarding; for Ross Macdonald's fiction was tied by innumerable threads to the life of Kenneth Millar.

The author's practice of weaving fact into fiction began early — as early as this pre-Archer private-eye tale from 1945. "Death by Water" swims with references to the 29-year-old Ken Millar's past and present, as well as with hints of books and events to come.

The Valeria Pueblo, with its bungalow cottages and live orchestra, is very like hotels where Ken and Margaret Millar stayed during the war. One of the tunes its musicians play, "In a Little Spanish Town," was a hit in the late 1920s, when 12-year-old Kenneth Millar lived in Winnipeg with his aunt and uncle, a man who kept a heavy handgun in the glovebox of his Packard. That man was a lifelong touchstone for Macdonald to the world of crime — as was this romantic old tune, heard in more than one Archer novel.

Another leitmotif throughout the Archer series is the detective's finely-tuned moral sense. His young predecessor Rogers also seems capable of precise ethical judgments.

Rogers agrees for instance that a fortune gained perhaps through duplicity has nonetheless been put to good use – for, as he's told, "It kept a sick woman in comfort and brought up a fatherless boy." (Here's another link to the story's author, who grew up virtually fatherless.) Yet Rogers knows the difference between good motives and evil acts. And, like the later Archer, he's as concerned with why such acts are done as with who did them. "The trouble's all over," Rogers says once the corpse is found. "I'm just trying to understand it."

The offhand remarks near the start of the story, then, about motives that fuel crime, lie at the heart of the matter. (Since they also plant clues to solving the mystery, they serve double-duty: another hallmark of Macdonald's technique.)

Note the difference between Rogers and his hotel-detective colleague, who gets up and leaves when the talk turns serious. Incurious of cause, Al Sablacan may someday feel its effect. If he so allows, he might become like Otto Sipe, the corrupt house dick in Macdonald's *The Far Side of the Dollar* (1964): living in the ruin of the once-grand Barcelona Hotel, where the bright dreams of 1945 have turned to dust, and the only guests are ghosts.

## NOTES

" 'I can think of few more complex critical enterprises' ": Macdonald, "Down These Streets a Mean Man Must Go," *Antaeus*, Spring/Summer 1977; reprinted in *Self-Portrait: Ceaselessly Into The Past* (Capra Press, 1981).

" 'hints of books and events to come' ": A "long, long circle" of the sort Millar savored in life, and Macdonald traced in fiction, can be drawn from the author's first private-eye story to his last p.i. novel thirty years later. Compare the death of Henry Ralston to Jacob Whitmore's in Macdonald's *The Blue Hammer* (Knopf, 1976): "Jacob Whitmore ... wasn't drowned in fresh water ... [He was] drowned in somebody's bathtub and chucked into the ocean afterwards."

# DEATH BY WATER

He was old, but he didn't look as if he were about to die. For a man of his age, which couldn't have been less than seventy, he was doing very well for himself. He was sitting at the bar buying drinks for three young sailors, and he was the life of the party in more than the financial sense. In the hour or so that I had been watching him, he must have had at least five martinis, and it was long past dinner time.

"The old man can carry his liquor," I said to Al.

"Mr. Ralston you mean? He's in here every night from eight to midnight, and it never seems to get him down. Of course some nights he gets too much, and I have to take him home and put him to bed. But next day he's bright as ever."

"He lives in the hotel, eh?"

Al Sablacan was the hotel detective of the Valeria Pueblo, which charged ten dollars a day and up and, unlike many Los Angeles hotels, was worth it. Until a couple of years ago, he had been a private detective, like me, but he had finally succumbed to varicose veins and the promise of security in his old age.

"He's our oldest inhabitant," Al said. "He's got a bungalow over near the swimming pool. Been there about ten years, I guess, him and his wife."

"He doesn't act married."

Mr. Ralston had left the bar and was leaning on the grand piano watching a dark Spanish-looking girl who strummed a guitar and sang pseudo-Latin songs in a sweet soprano. She was making eyes at Mr. Ralston in an exaggerated way which was intended to indicate that she was humoring the old man. Mr. Ralston was making faces at her, as if to express passionate delight.

"You show them, Mr. Ralston," one of the sailors said from the bar. "There's life in the old boy yet."

"Most assuredly," said Mr. Ralston, in rich and gracious tones. He gave a dollar to the singer, and she began to play "The Isle of Capri." Mr. Ralston danced in a small circle between the bar and the piano, making expansively romantic gestures. "Most assuredly," he repeated, with a winning smile which made everyone in the bar smile with him. "I am a little old dried up man, but I have a youthful heart."

"Isn't he a card?" Al said to me. "His wife's an invalid, and he must do a lot of worrying about her, but you'd never know it. He's a card."

There was a recess in the music, and Mr. Ralston approached our table on light feet and with a glowing face. "And how are you this evening?" he said to Al in tones of cultivated solicitude. "I don't believe I've met your friend. I do hope you'll overlook the absence of a tie. I neglected to put one on after dinner. I don't know what I was thinking of." He gave a little laugh of indulgence at his boyish recklessness.

"Joe Rogers, Mr. Ralston," Al said. "Joe's a private detective. We used to work together."

"How utterly fascinating," Mr. Ralston said. "Do you mind if I join you for a moment? I have some guests at the bar, but I can continue to act as host by remote control, so to speak." He ordered a round of drinks for us and the sailors at the bar. His martini disappeared like ether in air.

"I've often thought," he said to me, "that the life of a detective would be an intensely interesting one. I rather fancy myself as a student of human nature, but my studies have been somewhat academic, you might say. Isn't it true that one sees deepest into human nature in moments of strain, moments of crisis, the kind of moments that must be delightfully frequent in your own life, Mr. Rogers?"

"You see deep enough into certain aspects of human nature, I guess. Some of the things I've seen I'd just as soon forget."

"Such as?" said Mr. Ralston, his eyes bright with curiosity and alcohol.

"Hatred. Greed. Jealousy. The three emotions that cause most crime. Impersonal love of inflicting pain is a fourth."

"Your word 'impersonal' is interesting," Mr. Ralston said. "It implies a concept which has occurred to me, that sadism need not have a sexual content. Don't you think, though, that there may be a fifth possibility? Surely people have stolen, even killed, for love. Or would your definition of love exclude the more criminal passions?"

"This is where I came in," Al Sablacan said to me. "I've got to mosey around a bit, anyway, and see that everything's O.K."

"Hate is usually a more compelling motive than love," I said when Al had excused himself. "I think you may be right about sadism, though. May I ask what your business is, or was, Mr. Ralston?"

His thin expressive face registered a touch of shame. "I have to confess I never had any. Hence, perhaps, the abstraction of my psychological concepts. At one time, of course, I took a good deal of interest in my investments. In recent years much of my time has been devoted to my wife. She is not well, you see."

"I'm sorry to hear it."

"No, Mr. Rogers, Beatrice is not at all well. She is afflicted with a progressive muscular atrophy of the legs which has deprived her of all locomotive power. Her *thigh*, Mr. Rogers, her *thigh*, is no thicker than my forearm." He pushed up his shirt sleeve to exhibit his thin arm. "I often thank whatever gods there be that I am able to provide her with the best of loving care."

The singer returned to the piano bench and began to play. Mr. Ralston rose with courtly grace and excused himself. "There's a number I've been intending to request all evening. I'm extremely fond of it."

The musician collected another of Mr. Ralston's dollars and began to play "In a Little Spanish Town." Mr. Ralston hummed the tune with her, meanwhile conducting an imaginary orchestra with great verve.

"That's the spirit, Mr. Ralston," one of the sailors yelled. "If you had any hair you'd look exactly like Stokowski."

"Do not judge me by the hairiness or otherwise of my scalp," Mr. Ralston said joyously. "Judge me by my musical imagination."

I finished my drink and went out to the lobby to look for Al.

Whenever I visited him, Al had a cot set up for me in his ground floor room. At half-past twelve I was getting ready to roll into it, feeling pleasantly comatose from half a dozen bottles of beer. Al had finished his midnight rounds a few minutes before, and was taking off his tie in front of the mirror. There was a knock on the door, and he put his tie back on.

It was one of the Filipino bellhops. "Mr. Sablacan," he said excitedly when Al opened the door. "There are men swimming in the swimming pool. I told them they must not swim there at night, but they just laughed at me. I think you must come and kick them out."

"O.K., Louie. Are they guests?"

"I don't think so, Mr. Sablacan. Only Mr. Ralston."

"Mr. Ralston? Is he there?"

"Yessir. He is bouncing on the diving board."

"Want to come along, Joe?"

Mr. Ralston interested me, and I put my shirt back on and went along. He was standing on the board shining a big flashlight on the pool. Three young men were chasing each other around in the water, diving like porpoises and blowing like grampuses. When we got closer we could see that Mr. Ralston had nothing on but a pair of striped swimming trunks. The young men had nothing on at all.

"Hey, Mr. Ralston," Al shouted. "You can't do this."

"A lady with a lamp shall stand in the great history of the land," said Mr. Ralston.

"He's drunk as a lord," Al said to me. "I guess this is one of the nights I put him to bed."

"You'll have to tell your friends to get out of there," he said to Mr. Ralston.

"They are my guests," Mr. Ralston shouted severely. "They expressed a wish to go swimming, and naturally I indulged them."

"Get the hell out of there!" Al roared across the water. "I'll give you ten seconds and then I call the Shore Patrol."

The threat worked. The three sailors scrambled out of the pool and began to put on their clothes. Mr. Ralston came toward us, swinging the beam of the flashlight like a long luminous rod.

"You're not being very genial, Mr. Sablacan," he said in a disappointed tone. "Boys will be boys, you know. In fact, boys will be boys will be boys."

"You're no boy, Mr. Ralston. And it's time for you to be in bed."

"He's O.K.," said one of the sailors, a dark boy with a pleasant smile. "He said it was all right for us to come in here. We sort of got the idea that it was his private pool."

Mr. Ralston made a diversion. "Indeed I am O.K.," he said. "I am in superb physical shape." He beat with a thin fist on his withered chest, which was sparsely covered with grey hairs. "What is more, I take it to be one of my per-quisites to use this pool whenever I choose. My friends also."

The sailors had slipped away in the darkness. "Goodnight, Mr. Ralston," they called from the gate, and went out through the lobby. I helped Al to persuade Mr. Ralston to retire to his bungalow. We left him at the door and went to bed.

It was very early — scarcely dawn — when we were awakened by a knock at the door. Al rolled over and said sleepily, "Who is it?"

"It's Louie again, sorry Mr. Sablacan. We caught one of those sailors trying to get into the pueblo, and he says he wants to talk to you."

"O.K., O.K." Al rolled out of bed. "Hold him till I get there."

The dark young sailor was sitting in the lobby looking sheepish, with two bellhops standing over him.

"Where did you catch him?" Al said.

"He was trying to sneak through the lobby to the pueblo."

"My God!" Al yapped, his face bright red. "Don't tell me you were trying to go for another swim."

"I lost my I.D. card last night," the sailor said meekly. "I can't get back to the ship without it."

"How do I know that's true? We've had plenty of thieves around here."

"Mr. Ralston will vouch for me. I know his son."

"Mr. Ralston hasn't got a son."

"His stepson, I mean. Johnny Swain. We're on the same ship."

"We're not going to bother Mr. Ralston at this hour of the morning, but I'll give you one chance. We'll go and look for your I.D. card —"

"I think I must have dropped it when I took off my clothes."

It was there all right, lying in the grass beside the pool. James Denton, Seaman First Class, with his picture on it, looking sick.

"I should turn it in to the Shore Patrol and let you explain how you lost it," Al said.

"But you're not going to do that?"

"But I'm not going to do that. Just don't let me catch you taking advantage of Mr. Ralston, see?"

"I wouldn't take advantage of him," James Denton said. "He's a swell guy."

I had wandered to the edge of the pool and stood looking at the water, chlorine-green and smooth in the windless morning as polished agate. In the deepest corner I caught sight of something which shouldn't have been there. It was the pale body of a little old man, curled and still in his quiet corner like a foetus in alcohol.

James Denton had another swim after all. When he brought Mr. Ralston out of the pool, Mr. Ralston's temperature was that of the water.

"I guess this is partly my fault," James Denton said miserably. "We wouldn't let him come in last night, but I guess he came back after we left. He was a swell guy.

"Jeez, that chlorine gets the eyes," he said, wiping his eyes with the back of his hand. But he was very young, and I suspected that he was crying.

"Could Mr. Ralston swim?" I said to Al.

"I don't know, I never saw him swim. This is a terrible thing, Joe. So far as I know nobody ever drowned in this pool before."

He looked at Mr. Ralston and looked away. Mr. Ralston, with his blue face and red striped trunks, looked very small and weirdly pathetic on the grass. Al covered his face with a handkerchief.

"Well," he said, "I guess I better call Mr. Whittaker and the cops. Mr. Whittaker won't like this."

Mr. Whittaker, who owned the Valeria Pueblo, didn't like it. He was a small, spry, sharp-faced man with grey hair receding from hollow veined temples and hands that were never still. In his left cheek a tic jerked continually with an almost audible click. Whenever his cheek jerked Mr. Whittaker smiled to hide it, thus giving the impression of a rodent who periodically snarled.

He arrived simultaneously with the police and fox-trotted about in the grass, frequently snarling. "A most unfortunate accident," Mr. Whittaker said. "Clearly a most unfortunate accident. I trust the whole thing will be handled with a minimum of adverse publicity."

"It happens to all of us," the police lieutenant said. "I'd just as well bump this way as any other way."

James Denton and Al told the story of the swimming party while Mr. Whittaker rubbed his hands together in neurotic glee.

"Clearly a most unfortunate accident," Mr. Whittaker said.

"Looks as if you're right," the police lieutenant said. "But we'll have to take the body for autopsy."

Mr. Ralston was taken away in a grey blanket.

"Well, I guess that's that," Mr. Whittaker said frantically. "We've done all we can do."

"Who gets his money?" I said to Al.

"Mrs. Ralston does," said Mr. Whittaker. "Mrs. Ralston is practically the sole beneficiary. Poor woman."

"Who else profits by it?" I said.

"His brother Alexander, who is also a resident of Los Angeles, and his stepson John Swain. But only small bequests."

"How much?"

"Ten thousand each. His wife's nurse, Jane Lennon, was to get a *very* small bequest, five hundred dollars, I believe."

"How do you know?"

The last question had gone too far, and Mr. Whittaker came to. "Just who are *you*, my man?"

"The name is Rogers. I'm a detective."

"Excuse me, Mr. Rogers," Mr. Whittaker snarled ingratiatingly. "I'm a bit on edge this morning. Mr. Ralston was a very dear friend of mine."

"Don't apologize to me. I'm only a private detective, and I have nothing to do with this case. Unless, of course, the hotel wants to hire me to investigate it."

"I don't see that it requires investigation. It's clearly —"

"How much money did Mr. Ralston leave?"

"A great deal," Mr. Whittaker said reverently. "Well over a million."

"The accidental death of a millionaire always requires investigation," I said. "I work quietly. For twenty dollars a day." I was interested in the case and perfectly willing to make a little money out of my interest if I could.

"He's hot stuff, Mr. Whittaker," Al said. "Joe and I used to work together. He's cheap at the price."

"Naturally money is no object." Mr. Whittaker polished his nails on the front of his Harris tweed jacket, examined them, polished them again. "No object whatever. Very well, Rogers. See what you can find out."

"Twenty dollars a day in advance," I said.

He gave me twenty dollars. I said, "How do you happen to know the provisions of Mr. Ralston's will?"

"I witnessed it. He made no secret of it. He loved his wife, and he wanted her to have his money."

"Did she love him?"

"Of course she loved him. Mrs. Ralston is a very fine and loyal woman. In spite of her grievous affliction, she made the old man an excellent wife."

"How old is she?"

"In her early forties. I can't see the point in these questions. I hope you're not going to stir up any trouble?"

"The trouble's all over," I said. "I'm just trying to understand it."

James Denton, the sailor, reminded us that he had been sitting silently on the grass ever since the police left. "Is it all right if I go?" he said. "I'm supposed to get back to the ship at San Pedro at nine, and I don't think I'll make it."

I said, "You're a friend of Mr. Ralston's stepson John Swain?"

He stood up and said, "Yessir."

"Why didn't John come along with you last night?"

"He was restricted to the ship, because he was absent over leave at Pearl. I was here before with John, and Mr. Ralston said he'd be glad to see me any time."

"If you're restricted to the ship, there's no way you can get off, is that right?"

"Yessir. There are guards on the gangways, and you have to report to the Master-at-Arms."

"What ship are you on?"

"APA 237."

"Is there a phone aboard?"

"Yessir." He gave me the number.

"If we need you we'll get in touch with you. Were the other two boys from the same ship?"

"Yessir." He gave me their names and left.

"Better call John Swain on the APA 237 and tell him to come here," I said to Al. "If they won't let him off, Mr. Whittaker will verify it."

"Yes, of course," said Mr. Whittaker, who seemed happier when he had no decisions to make.

Al went back to the main building to phone, and I asked Mr. Whittaker which was the Ralstons' bungalow. He pointed to a long low stucco building, half hidden in flowering shrubbery, about fifty yards from the pool.

"What's the setup in there?" I said.

"What do you mean?"

"How many rooms? How big a ménage? Sleeping arrangements and so on."

"Three bedrooms, a living room, and a kitchenette. Two bathrooms, one off Mr. Ralston's bedroom, the other shared by Mrs. Ralston and her nurse. Mrs. Ralston has a full-time nurse, of course. I don't know whether you knew she was a cripple."

"Yes, I know. The rooms are interconnecting, I suppose?"

"All but the bathrooms and kitchenette open on the central hallway. I could draw you a plan —"

"That's hardly necessary. I thought I'd just go and take a look. And isn't it about time somebody told Mrs. Ralston what happened to her husband?"

"By Jove, I forgot about that." He glanced at an octagonal platinum wristwatch which said seven-thirty. After a pause during which his cheek was active, he said, "I think I should consult her physician before breaking the news to Mrs. Ralston. In view of her physical condition. Excuse me."

He trotted stiffly away. I sauntered down the concrete walk to the Ralston bungalow. With all the Venetian blinds down it looked impassive yet vulnerable, like a face with closed eyes. For some reason I was leery of pressing the bell push, as if it might be a signal for something to jump out at me.

What jumped out at me was a very pretty brunette in her ripe late twenties and a fresh white nurse's uniform.

"Please don't make any noise," she said. "Mrs. Ralston is sleeping."

*You look as if you could do with some sleep,* I thought. There were blue-grey rings under her eyes and the flesh of her face drooped.

I said, "Miss Lennon?"

"Yes?" She stepped outside onto the little porch and closed the door behind her. I noticed that the concrete floor of the porch sloped up to the doorstep and down to the walk. Of course, Mrs. Ralston would have a wheelchair.

"My name is Rogers. Mr. Whittaker has hired me to investigate the death of Mr. Ralston."

"What?" The drooping flesh around her eyes and mouth slanted upward in lines of painful astonishment.

"Mr. Ralston was drowned in the swimming pool last night. Can you throw any light on the accident?"

"My God. This will kill Mrs. Ralston."

"It killed Mr. Ralston."

She looked at me narrowly. "When?"

"One or two in the morning, I'd say. The police will be able to give a better estimate when they complete the autopsy."

"I can't imagine," she said.

"You didn't see or hear anything?"

"Not a thing. Mrs. Ralston and I went to bed before midnight and slept right through. I just got up a few minutes ago. This will be a terrible shock to her."

"Do you sleep in the same room with her?"

"Adjoining rooms. I keep the door open at night in case she needs me for anything."

"Where did Mr. Ralston sleep?"

"His room is across the hall from ours. How on earth did he fall in?"

"That's what I'm trying to find out. Did he go in for swimming?"

"I've seen him swim. But he hardly went in at all the last few years. He was getting pretty old."

"How old?"

"Seventy-three."

"Thanks," I said. "Don't say anything to Mrs. Ralston just yet. Mr. Whittaker has gone to call her doctor."

"I won't say anything."

She went back into the bungalow, moving as quietly as a cat. I found my way to the dining room, where Al was just finishing his breakfast.

"I talked to John Swain," he said. "He's coming right over from Pedro in a taxi."

"How did he take it?"

"He was upset all right. But I guess it didn't floor him."

"Could anyone have gotten into the pueblo last night after we left Mr. Ralston?"

"We locked the gates at midnight. After that the only way to get in is through the lobby, and there's always somebody on duty there. Nobody but a guest or an employee could get in, unless he climbed the wall."

"Would that be hard?"

"You saw it." The wall was solid brick, about eight feet high, and topped with iron spikes. "Why? You're not thinking somebody got in and killed the old man?"

"It sounds impossible, doesn't it? But a man has to be pretty drunk to go swimming by himself after midnight at the age of seventy-three. Drunker than Mr. Ralston was."

"I don't know," Al said.

After I had eaten a quick breakfast we went to look for Mr. Whittaker. He was in his office sitting on the corner of the desk and swinging a leg in time like a metronome.

"Dr. Wiley will be here in a few minutes," he said. "He said we'd better wait for him."

I told him the nurse's story, that she'd slept through the night and hadn't heard a thing. Then Dr. Wiley arrived, a large cheerful man dressed for golf but carrying a medical bag.

"I don't anticipate any serious reaction," Dr. Wiley said. "But it's just as well to be prepared. There's no telling how a woman who is not at all well will react to a shock of this nature."

"I dread this," Mr. Whittaker said. "This is going to be an ordeal."

When we reached the bungalow Mrs. Ralston was sunning herself in front of it in a wheelchair, her legs swathed in a steamer rug. Even under the rug the lower half of her body looked pathetically feeble, but from the waist up she seemed at first glance to be a healthy woman of forty. Her bosom was impressive and her shoulders were handsome in a light linen blouse. Her face was strong and beautiful in a bold and striking way, but there were shadows in it. Until now, it seemed to me, she had held out against her disease, but now she was approaching the point of surrender. There were daubs of grey in her carefully dressed brown hair.

Yet she waived gaily at her doctor and showed her white even teeth in a smile. "I wasn't expecting you this morning," she said.

Al and I stood back and pretended to look at the trees while Whittaker and Dr. Wiley walked up to her without speaking. The nurse stood in the background looking worried.

"I have bad news for you," Dr. Wiley said. "Mr. Ralston —" He hesitated.

"Why, Mr. Ralston is sleeping in his room." She turned her head to the nurse and I saw the tendons in her neck. "Isn't Mr. Ralston still asleep, Jane?"

Jane bit her lower lip, which was full and purplish like a plum.

"Mr. Ralston is dead," the doctor said. "He drowned in the pool last night."

Mrs. Ralston's hands closed on the arms of her wheelchair. She sat bold upright, supported by her straining arms. The bony structure of her face became apparent, and the shadows there deepened.

"Poor Henry," she said. "How did it happen?"

Before anyone could answer she fell backward and covered her face with her long and graceful hands.

A young man in neat sailor blues appeared at the gate and came running across the grass towards us. He went by us like a blue streak, half-kneeled by the wheelchair and took hold of Mrs. Ralston's shoulders. "Mother," he said. "How are you feeling, darling?"

"Johnny," said Mrs. Ralston, removing her hands from her face, where the convulsions of grief gave way to the convulsions of maternal feeling. "My dear boy, I'm so glad you've come."

"Yes, how *are* you feeling, Mrs. Ralston?" said Dr. Wiley. "I think I should take your pulse."

He and Mr. Whittaker hovered around her for a few minutes more, attending to her physical comfort and telling her the details of her husband's death. Then they moved away to rejoin us, leaving her alone with her son and her nurse.

"An amazing woman," said Dr. Wiley. "She took it better than I could have expected."

"She has courage," said Mr. Whittaker.

"Courage is her middle name," said Dr. Wiley. "You'd never think to look at her that she has no more than three months to live."

"Three months to live?" I said.

"I've consulted with the leading specialists in the country," Dr. Wiley said. "Amyotrophic lateral sclerosis is a progressive disease, and can never be fully arrested. She can't live more than three months, and she knows it. But what a stiff upper lip she maintains!"

Before we entered the hotel I looked back at Mrs. Ralston. Johnny Swain was still half-kneeling beside her, supporting her head on his shoulder. The nurse was still standing in the background, looking worried.

The police lieutenant who was handling the case was waiting in the lobby. He wanted to interview Mrs. Ralston and her nurse, and line up the other witnesses for the inquest.

"Is the autopsy completed?" I asked him.

"Dr. Shantz is working on it now."

"What's the dope so far?"

"A straight case of drowning. What did you expect?"

"A straight case of drowning," I said.

I took Al aside and told him, "I'm going down to the police lab and talk to Dr. Shantz. There are a couple of things you can be doing. Check Johnny Swain's alibi. Find out for sure whether he was aboard his ship last night. And see if you can find anything to shake the nurse's story that she spent the night in bed. She didn't look to me as if she did."

"Right," said Al, who seemed glad to have something to do.

I took my car out of the parking lot across the street and drove downtown to see Dr. Shantz. He was in his office when I got there, having completed the autopsy, but he still had on his surgical whites. With his domelike belly and three chins, he looked more like the popular idea of a chef than a medico-legal expert.

He said to me when I came in, "I didn't know you were interested in this cadaver, Joe."

"I'm always interested. I'm an occupational necrophile."

"I've got a beautiful Lysol burn in the back room. Want to see it?"

"Not just now, thanks. The hotel hired me to check on the Ralston accident. They don't like people drowning in their swimming pool. No signs of foul play, I suppose?"

"None whatever."

"Heart failure?"

"Nope, except in the sense that the heart usually stops when you die. The old man drowned. His lungs were full of water."

"No foreign substance of any kind?"

"You can't make a murder case out of this one, Joe. Mr. Ralston was killed by pure city water. I applied Gettler's test to the blood content of the heart, and that's definite."

"When did he die?"

"It's hard to say exactly. His stomach was empty, except for some water, and he ate dinner at seven. His temperature was almost down to the temperature of the water. Between two and three in the morning, I'd say."

"That was about my guess," I said. "Thanks."

"Don't mention it. That Lysol burn will still be here tomorrow if you want to see it."

"Thanks again," I said and went out. I was almost certain now that a murder had been committed, since I'd never known Shantz to make a professional mistake. I decided to go and see Mr. Ralston's brother Alexander. He got ten thousand dollars out of Mr. Ralston's death. How badly did he need ten thousand dollars?

I found him in the phone book and drove to his address, a one-story stucco house on a middling street in South Los Angeles. He answered the doorbell, a scrawny man in his sixties with thin grey hair and stooping shoulders. His thick glasses made his eyes seem unnaturally large and solemn.

He spoke solemnly. "What can I do for you, sir?"

"Rogers is the name. I'm investigating your brother's death —"

"A sad affair. Johnny Swain phoned me not long ago. I didn't realize, however, that it was under police investigation."

"I'm working for the hotel. All they want to do is make sure it was an accident. You may be able to give me some information about your brother's habits?"

"Won't you step inside? I haven't seen much of Henry in recent years, but I'll tell you what I can. Don't get the notion that we weren't on good terms. We were. You may know that he left me ten thousand dollars in his will?"

He led me into the living room and waved me towards a shabby chesterfield. Except for the shelves of books which lined the walls, everything in the room was shabby. In his collarless shirt and drooping trousers, Alexander Ralston suited the room. I wondered if he was a lifelong victim of primogeniture.

He saw me looking around the room and said, "I'm afraid things are in rather a mess. I do my own housekeeping, you know. I won't attempt to deny that for a retired teacher like myself that ten thousand dollars will come in very handily, very handily indeed."

"You say you hadn't seen a great deal of your brother in recent years?"

"That's quite true. Our interests differed, you see. I like to think of myself as something of an intellectual, and Henry was by way of being a hedonist. I won't accuse him of having no intellectual interests, but they weren't sustained. In a word, his money spoilt him for the life of the spirit."

"Where did he get it?"

"His money? Of course, you must be struck by the contrast between our ways of life. It was really quite a comic situation — I pride myself on being able to laugh at it still, though in a way I was the butt of the joke." He smiled wanly and stroked his one day's beard.

I began to suspect that I was dealing with an eccentric. "I don't quite get the point," I said.

"Naturally you don't. I haven't told you the situation. Henry and I had a very devout aunt who married well and in the course of time became a very wealthy and devout widow. Henry had never been given to religiosity, but Aunt Martha cracked the whip of gold over him, so to speak, and persuaded him to enter the church when he was in his early twenties. I was a freshman in college at the time, and I was a militant atheist. I still am, sir. Anyway, Aunt Martha left all her money to Henry.

"It's just as well, I suppose," he said after a pause. "Overmuch money would have suited ill with the austerities of moral philosophy and metaphysics. Still, that ten thousand dollars will come in very handily."

"I understand that Mrs. Ralston will get the bulk of his fortune."

"Of course she will. And it's only fitting. She married him for that purpose, I believe."

"How long had they been married?"

"Ten years. She was about thirty at the time, and a very pretty piece — I use the word in its seventeenth-century sense. Within six months of their marriage she had become a hopeless invalid. I've suspected, perhaps without justification, that Mrs. Ralston knew at the time of their marriage that she had the disease, and deliberately inveigled Henry into it. He was really an innocent-hearted man. She was a widow without means, you see, and had a young son to support. Even if that is the case, however, I don't begrudge her the money. It kept a sick woman in comfort and brought up a fatherless boy, and thus served a useful purpose, don't you think?"

I said, "Yes."

"There's one other thing," Alexander Ralston said, his exaggerated eyes regarding me blandly through his glasses. "This is an absurd hypothesis, but I think I should introduce it. Assuming that I was intending to kill my brother for his money, I should certainly have waited a few months. His death at the present time has netted me ten thousand dollars. After Mrs. Ralston's death, which you may or may not know is imminent, Henry's death would have netted me incomparably more. His entire fortune, in fact."

I am not easily embarrassed, but I was embarrassed. "I never thought of such a thing," I said unconvincingly.

"Please don't be uncomfortable. It's your duty to think of such things. But now if you'll excuse me, I have some work to do."

I told him it had been a pleasure to meet him, and went away.

When I got back to the Valeria Pueblo, Al was in his room reading a newspaper. He put it down when I opened the door.

"The accident didn't make much of a splash," he said. "Say, that's a crack, isn't it? But I notice there's nobody in swimming in the pool today."

"There will be tomorrow. In a week it'll be forgotten. What about John Swain's alibi?"

"He was on the ship all night," Al said. "He played poker till 4 a.m., and has four buddies to prove it. I talked to one on the phone."

"That lets him out, then. Did you get anything on Jane Lennon?"

He winked and smiled lasciviously. "You're damn right. One of the black girls who cleans the bungalows gave me the straight dope on her. I knew that dame had too much to be going to waste."

"Spill it."

"She's got a boy friend in one of the other bungalows. Her racket is to wait until Mrs. Ralston goes to sleep, and then slip out for a few hours. Mrs. Ralston takes sleeping powders, see, so the nurse thought she was safe enough. But she was supposed to be on twenty-four hour duty, and she was taking a chance."

"Where was Jane Lennon last night?"

"With her boyfriend. The black girl saw her going back to her own bungalow just before dawn. But I don't see how you're going to use that against her. It gives her a better alibi than she had before."

I said, "Is Mrs. Ralston's wheelchair self-propelling? I mean can she move it herself?"

"Sure, if she wants to. But the nurse usually pushes her. My God, you're not suspecting Mrs. Ralston now?"

I said nothing.

"You're a sap if you are," Al said. "She had no motive. The dame's going to be dead in a couple of months."

"That's right," I said. "Let's go and see Mrs. Ralston."

"Look here, you take it easy," Al said. "You'll make trouble for both of us."

"The widow should be informed that her husband was murdered," I said. "I'm going to inform the widow."

Mrs. Ralston, John Swain, and Jane Lennon were sitting at an outside table in the patio. They had just finished their lunch, and a waiter was removing their debris. When he had glided away with his loaded tray, I stepped up to the table with Al beside me.

"May we join you for a moment?" I said.

"Why certainly." Mrs. Ralston looked up at me brightly, and with a movement of her right hand turned her wheelchair in a quarter circle.

I sat down facing her and said, "Last night about a quarter to one Mr. Sablacan and I left your husband at the door of your bungalow and he presumably went to bed. Since he had been drinking he probably fell into a deep alcoholic slumber. An hour or so later he was drowned. This morning I found him in the swimming pool."

"I know those things," Mrs. Ralston said. "Is there any point in repeating them to me?"

"This is very painful for my mother," John Swain said. "I'll have to ask you to put a stop to it." He dropped his cigarette on the tiles and ground it angrily under his heel.

"I have reason to believe," I said, "that Mr. Ralston was

not drowned in the swimming pool."

Mrs. Ralston slumped backward and covered her face with her hands. John Swain stood up and leaned across the table towards me looking as if he would like to bite me.

"This is too much!" he said. "I'll see Mr. Whittaker about this." He marched away into the hotel.

"O.K.," I said to Jane Lennon. "Take her away. I'd just as soon be telling it to the police."

Mrs. Ralston removed her hands. She looked old, and I felt sorry for her. I felt sorrier for Mr. Ralston.

"The police?" she said.

"Somebody drowned him in the bathtub," I said. "He was very light."

Mrs. Ralston picked up a glass ashtray from the table, and threw it at my face. It struck my forehead and made a gash there. While I was dabbing at the blood with a handkerchief, Mrs. Ralston called me many unusual names in a loud voice which attracted the attention of everyone in the patio. Jane Lennon wheeled her away. I was glad to see her go, because Mrs. Ralston's face had become very old and ugly.

Mr. Whittaker came running out of the hotel with John Swain at his heels.

"What's all this!" he cried.

"Call the police again," I said. "Mrs. Ralston seems ready to confess."

An hour later I was sitting with Al in his room sipping my first beer of the day and wishing away a headache.

"You took a hell of a chance," Al said.

"No, I didn't. I made no accusations. All I said was that somebody had drowned him in the bathtub. Mrs. Ralston said the rest."

"I still think it's lucky for you she broke down and confessed. You didn't have any evidence."

"I had one piece of evidence," I said. "The whole case

hung on it. The water in Mr. Ralston's lungs was pure city water. He couldn't have inhaled it in the pool, because the pool water has a good deal of chlorine in it. A bathtub was practically the only alternative."

"I don't see how she did it," Al said.

"Morally, it's hard to see. Murder always is. Physically, it was feasible enough. He weighed scarcely a hundred pounds. There was nothing the matter with her arms and shoulders, and a wheelchair can be a pretty useful vehicle. She simply wheeled him to the bathtub, held his face under water until he stopped breathing, wheeled him out to the pool, and dumped him in. It must have been difficult, and she stood a chance of being caught at it, but she hadn't much to lose."

"And nothing at all to gain. That's what I don't get. What good is a million dollars to a dame that's going to die any day?"

"She wanted to leave it to her son," I said. "He'd have been cut off from all that money if she had died before her husband. Ever since the doctors told her she was going to die, she must have been waiting for her chance. She probably caught on to the nurse's trick long ago, and bided her time, waiting to use it. That swimming party last night gave her her opportunity. Mother love is a wonderful thing."

I thought of another wonderful thing then, and I began to laugh though it wasn't very funny. In California a murderess can't inherit her victim's property. So Johnny Swain is still as far away from a million dollars as the rest of us.

# STRANGERS IN TOWN

# STRANGERS IN TOWN

## Preface by Tom Nolan

Like all Ross Macdonald's fiction, this tale was inspired by, or incorporated details from, Ken Millar's life. One event that sparked "Strangers in Town" was a February 1950 dinner party at the Palm Springs home of movie-studio head Darryl F. Zanuck, to which the Millars were taken by Bennett Cerf (Margaret's publisher), who was staying in the nearby desert resort of La Quinta. When a medical thermometer packed in a suitcase for this trip was found reading 107°, a clue was born.

And maybe Darryl Zanuck — who made a show of having himself publicly shaved in the presence of his guests — plays a cameo role in "Strangers," cast against type as the gangster Durano, dwarfed by his baronial house and with "two days' beard on his chin, like motheaten grey plush."

Other characters receive a share of Millar's own experience, as the author finds common emotional cause with citizens superficially unlike him. Archer's African-American client, like Ken Millar, is an ex-schoolteacher. Like Millar — who grew up poor and got to college only by dint of his father's $2,000 in life insurance — the Hispanic lawyer Santana "had come up the long hard way, and remembered every step." The religious motto on the wall in Mrs. Norris's house is straight out of Kenneth Millar's childhood.

The vignette of a teenager or young man being taught to dance by an older girl (as Lucy teaches Alex) occurs so often in Millar manuscripts and notebooks, it surely must have figured importantly in the author's past.

Another object purloined from Millar's history is the bolo knife sent from the Philippines by Alex's chief petty officer father. It's a duplicate of the souvenir Lt. j.g. Ken Millar sought in those islands in January of 1946, when he wrote his daughter Linda from the *U.S.S. Shipley Bay:* "I've been trying to find a good bolo knife to hang over our mantel." The next day he reported to his wife: "I went ashore ... I bought a bolo knife to hang on the wall ... for $1.50 ..."

The "Mickey" whom Durano has been sent to neutralize would be West Coast operator Mickey Cohen. The syndicate's caution "this year especially" is due to the Kefauver hearings on organized crime.

L.A. columnist's legman Morris Cramm appeared in the 1950 Archer novel *The Drowning Pool.* Reviewer Anthony Boucher found him delightful and urged Millar to use him again. Macdonald obliged.

## NOTES

" 'I've been trying to find a good bolo knife' ": Kenneth to Linda Millar, January 8, 1946, The Kenneth Millar Papers, Special Collections and Archives, UC Irvine Libraries.

" 'I went ashore' ": Kenneth to Margaret Millar, January 9, 1946, The Kenneth Millar Papers, Special Collections and Archives, UC Irvine Libraries..

# STRANGERS IN TOWN

"My son is in grave trouble," the woman said.

I asked her to sit down, and after a moment's hesitation she lowered her weight into the chair I placed for her. She was a large Negro woman, clothed rather tightly in a blue linen dress which she had begun to outgrow. Her bosom was rising and falling with excitement, or from the effort of climbing the flight of stairs to my office. She looked no older than forty, but the hair that showed under her blue straw hat was the color of steel wool. Perspiration furred her upper lip.

"About your son?" I sat down behind my desk, the possible kinds of trouble that a Negro boy could get into in Los Angeles running like a newsreel through my head.

"My son has been arrested on suspicion of murder." She spoke with a schoolteacher's precision. "The police have had him up all night, questioning him, trying to force a confession out of him."

"Where is he held? Lincoln Heights?"

"In Santa Teresa. We live there. I just came down on the bus to see if you could help me. There are no private detectives in Santa Teresa."

"He have a lawyer?"

"Mr. Santana. He recommended you to me, Mr. Archer."

"I see." Santana I knew by name and reputation as a leader of minority groups in Southern California. He had come up the long hard way, and remembered every step. "Well, what are the facts?"

"Before I go over them in detail, I would like to be assured that you'll take the case."

"I'd like to be assured that your son isn't guilty."

"He isn't. They have nothing against him but circumstances."

"Not many murder cases depend on witnesses, Mrs. —"

"Norris, Genevieve Norris. My son's name is Alex, after his father." The modulation of her voice suggested that Alex senior was dead. "Alex is entering his sophomore year in college," she added with pride.

"What does Santana think?"

"Mr. Santana knows that Alex is innocent. He'd have come to you himself, except that he's busy trying to have him freed. He thinks the woman may have committed suicide —"

"It was a woman, then."

"She was my boarder. I'll tell you honestly, Mr. Archer, Alex had grown fond of her. Much too fond. The woman was older than him — than he — and different. A different class of person from Alex. I was going to give her notice when she — died."

"How did she die?'

"Her throat was cut."

Mrs. Norris laid a genteel brown hand on her bosom, as if to quiet its surge. A plain gold wedding band was sunk almost out of sight in the flesh of one of her fingers. The hand came up to her lip and dashed away the moisture there. "I found her myself, last midnight. Her terrible breathing woke me. I thought maybe she was sick or — intoxicated. By the time I reached her she was dead on the floor, in her blood. Do you know how I felt, Mr. Archer?" She leaned towards me with the diffident and confiding charm of her race, her eyes deeply shadowed by the brim of her hat: "As if all the things I had dreaded for myself and Alex, when we were going from city to city during the depression, trying to find a living, in Buffalo, Detroit, Chicago. As if they'd suddenly come true, in my own house. When I saw Lucy in her blood." Her voice broke like a cello string.

"Who was Lucy?" I asked her after a pause.

"Lucy Deschamps is her name. She claimed to be a Creole from New Orleans. Alex was taken in, he's a romantic boy, but I don't know. She was common."

"Weapon?"

She looked at me blankly.

"If it might have been suicide, the weapon was there."

"Yes, of course. The weapon was there. It was a long native knife. My husband sent it from the Philippines before his ship was sunk. Mr. Norris was a chief petty officer in the Navy." Her unconscious panic was pushing her off the point, into the security and respectability of her past.

I brought her back to the point: "And where was Alex?"

"Sleeping in his room. He has a room of his own. A college student needs a room of his own. When I screamed, he came running in in his pyjamas. He let out a cry and lay down beside her. I couldn't get him up. When the policemen came, he was blood from head to foot. He said he was responsible for her death, he was really wild. They took him away." Bowed forward in her chair like a great black Rachel, she had forgotten her careful speech and her poise. Her shadowed eyes were following the image of her son into the shadows.

I rose and fetched her a drink from the water-cooler in the corner of the room. "We can drive up to Santa Teresa together," I said, "if that suits you. I want to hear more about Lucy."

She gulped the water and stood up. She was almost as tall as I was, and twice as imposing.

"Of course. You're a kind man, Mr. Archer."

I took the inland route, over Cahuenga Pass. It wasn't built for speed, but the sparseness of traffic gave me a chance to listen. As we moved north out of the valley, the heat eased off. The withered September hills were a moving backdrop to the small sad romance of Alex Norris and Lucy.

She had come to the house in a taxi about a month before, a handsome light brown woman of twenty-five or so, well-dressed and well-spoken. She preferred to stay in a private home, she said, because all but the worst hotels in Santa Teresa were closed to her. Mrs. Norris gave her the spare room, the one in the front of the house with the separate entrance, which she sometimes rented out when she could find a suitable tenant. The rent-money would help with Alex's tuition.

Miss Deschamps was a peaceful little soul, or so she seemed. She ate most of her meals with the family, almost never went out, spent most of her evenings quietly in her room with the portable radio she had brought along with her. She seldom spoke about herself, except to let it be understood that she had been a lady's maid in some very good families. But she made Mrs. Norris nervous. The landlady felt that her boarder was under tension, planning her words and actions in order not to give anything away. She seemed afraid, almost as if she were in hiding from someone or something. It put everyone under a strain.

The strain became severe when Mrs. Norris discovered one day that Lucy was a solitary drinker. It happened quite by accident, as she was cleaning the room during one of Lucy's rare walks. She opened up a bureau drawer to change the paper lining, and found it half full of empty whisky bottles. And then she learned, in conversation with Alex, that Alex had been serving as Lucy's errand-boy, bringing her nightly pints from the liquor store. That she had rewarded Alex by teaching him to dance, alone in her room, to the music of the portable radio. That Lucy, to put it briefly (as Mrs. Norris did), had been transforming her God-fearing household into a dancehall-saloon, her son into God knew what.

This had been on a Monday, three days before. When Mrs. Norris had threatened to evict her tenant, Lucy promised in tears to be good, if only she might stay. Alex announced that if Lucy were forced to leave, he would go with her. Now, in a sense, he had.

"What did he mean by saying that he was responsible?"

"Alex? When?" Mrs. Norris shifted uncomfortably in the seat beside me.

"Last night. You said he told the police that he was responsible for her death."

"Did I say that? You must have misunderstood me." But she wouldn't meet my eyes.

It was just as well, because I almost missed the first Santa Teresa stoplight. I braked the car to a screaming stop, half over the white line. "All right, I misunderstood you. Let me get it straight about the weapon. Had it been lying around the house?"

"Yes."

"In Lucy's room?"

"I don't know where it was, Mr. Archer. It might have been anywhere in the house. It was usually on the mantel in the living room, but Lucy could easily get it if she wanted to do herself an injury."

"Why would she want to?"

The light changed, and I turned right, in the direction of the courthouse.

"Because she was afraid. I told you that."

"But you don't know what of?"

"No."

"Her past is simply a blank? She didn't tell you anything, except that she was a lady's maid from New Orleans?"

"No."

"Or why she came to you?"

"Oh, I know why she came to my house. She was referred. Dr. Benning referred her to me. She went to him as a patient."

"What was the matter with her?"

"I don't know. She didn't seem ill to me, the way she carried on."

"Maybe I'd better talk to this doctor first. Did you tell the police that he sent Lucy to you?"

She was watching the bright stucco street as if it might narrow at any moment into an arc-lit alley, ambushed at each end. "I didn't tell them anything much." Her voice was glum.

Following her directions, I drove across the railroad tracks which cut through the center of town. The double band of steel was like a social equator dividing Santa Teresa roughly into lighter and darker hemispheres. Dr. Benning's house, which also contained his office, stood in the lower latitudes, a block above the station, two blocks off the main street. It was a grey old three-storied building standing in a block of run-down shops. The faded sign on the wall beside the front door, Samuel Benning, M.D., seemed large, even for California.

A young woman opened the door as I pulled up to the curb. She had straight black hair, trimmed short, and black-rimmed harlequin spectacles that gave her face an Asiatic cast. Though her body looked rather lumpy in an ill-fitting white uniform, I noticed that her waist and ankles were narrow.

"Who's she?" I asked the woman beside me.

"I never saw her before. Must be a new receptionist."

I got out and approached her. "Is Dr. Benning in?"

"He's just going out to lunch." Her spectacles or the blue eyes behind them glittered coldly in the sun.

"It's rather important. A woman has been killed. I understand that she was one of his patients."

"She boarded with me." Mrs. Norris had come up behind me. "Miss Lucy Deschamps."

"Lucy Deschamps?" The chill spread from her eyes across her face, drawing her unpainted mouth into a thin blue line.

"I don't recall the name."

"The doctor probably will." I started up the walk that crossed the narrow yard.

As if of its own accord, her body moved to bar my way. She spoke on an indrawn breath: "How was she killed?"

"Cut throat."

"How awful." She turned away, towards the house. Her feet groped for the verandah steps like a blind woman's.

Dr. Benning was in the entrance hall, brushing a felt hat that badly needed brushing. He was a thin, high-shouldered man of indeterminate age. A fringe of reddish hair grew like withering grass around the pink desert expanse of his bald scalp.

"Good morning." His pale eyes shifted from me to the Negro woman. "Why, hello, Mrs. Norris. What's the trouble?"

"Trouble is the right word, doctor. The boarder you sent me last month, she was killed. Alex has been arrested."

"I'm sorry to hear it, naturally. But I didn't send you anyone last month. Did I?"

"That's what I told her," the receptionist put in. "I never heard the name Lucy Deschamps."

"Just a minute, Miss Tennent. I think I remember now. She probably came here on a Wednesday, when you were off. I may have forgotten to make a note of her visit." He turned to Mrs. Norris, who blocked the doorway. "Was she that light-brown woman from San Francisco?"

"I don't know where she was from. All she said was that you sent her to me. She came to my house in a taxi and I let her move in." There was a veiled accusation in Mrs. Norris' tone: no doctor should send a potential murderee to a respectable landlady.

"You can hardly say I sent her to you. She'd just got off the train, and was looking for a place to stay, and I may have mentioned your place as a possibility. What's this about Alex being arrested?"

Mrs. Norris told him. The receptionist stood flat against the wall at his elbow, steadily watching his face.

The doctor clucked sympathetically. "Too bad. He's a fine boy. I'll go down and talk to the D.A. if you like." He turned to me again: "You a detective?"

"A private one. I'm working for Mrs. Norris."

"Found out anything?"

"I hoped I would from you. Where the woman came from, what she was doing here, what was the matter with her."

"She came here in the middle of the afternoon, said she got off the San Francisco train. Just a minute, I'll check my records." He placed his hat on his head, dropping ten years.

I followed him into the waiting room, where he rummaged in a battered filing cabinet behind the receptionist's desk. The rest of the furniture was equally dilapidated. There was a worn linoleum rug on the floor.

He looked up with a deprecatory smile: "I'm sorry, I have so many cash patients, I don't keep complete records. I do remember this woman though. She had some kind of female trouble, a slight irregularity. She'd blown it up in her head into a malignant disease. I set her mind at rest as well as I could, and gave her a hormone prescription, and that was all there was to it. Typical hypochondriac."

"She wasn't seriously ill, then."

"I'd stake my reputation on it." The room mocked his words, and he grinned sheepishly. His teeth were poor. "Of course it's possible," he added slowly, "that she didn't accept my reassurances, and killed herself out of pure funk. In any case, it's certainly rough on Jenny."

"Mrs. Norris is a friend of yours?"

"Yes, I'd call her a friend. She's often nursed patients for me, in their homes. Jenny's not a trained nurse, but she's a dependable woman. Used to teach school in Detroit. Her son's quite brilliant, I hear. Scholarship student. He's Jenny's pride and joy."

"Evidently. You say the woman came here on a Wednesday."

"It must have been —" He consulted the desk-calendar "— Wednesday, August 16, I'd say. Five weeks ago yesterday."

"Thanks, Doctor. One other thing. Would you class her as a suicidal type?"

"I didn't talk to her for very long, and I'm no psychiatrist. All I can say is that it's possible. She was prone to phobias, certainly."

I left him standing in the unsuccessful room, hatted and ill-at-ease in his own house. Miss Tennent and Mrs. Norris were close together in the hallway, talking in low tones about Lucy's death. The white-uniformed girl leaned towards the dark woman with an eagerness that almost amounted to sickness. When I brushed past her she shied away.

Santana was closeted with a Superior Court judge in the judge's chambers. The District Attorney was holding himself incommunicado in his office. The Deputy D.A. I talked to wouldn't say a word about the case, except to indicate that Alex was still in jail, for all kinds of excellent reasons. I finally found the Sheriff eating lunch in a lunch-bar across the street from the courthouse.

Sheriff Kerrigan was a big middle-aged man in a rumpled business suit. He was reasonable, as elected police officials often tended to be. My connection with Santana, and Santana's influence on the Mexican and Negro vote, were no disadvantage at all. He took me to see the body at the morgue.

This occupied the rear of a fly-specked mortuary a short walk from the courthouse. The dead woman lay on a marble-topped table under a sheet. The Sheriff removed the sheet, and switched on a naked light. I looked down into wide blank eyes. Lucy's skin was shriveled and jaundiced from loss of blood, which had wasted through a gaping slash in her neck. Her orange silk pyjamas were heavily stained. I noticed before I looked away that the silk was real. She had red mules on her feet.

"Not pretty," Kerrigan said. "I don't like it any better than you do."

"Where did she come from?"

"I'll be frank with you," he answered heavily. "I haven't the slightest idea. The city identification officer is stumped —"

"No kidding, Sheriff."

"Absolutely not. There's nothing in her room to give us a lead. Repeat, nothing. No laundry marks, no social security card, no labels on the clothes that tell us anything, nothing written down. It's possible she couldn't write, I don't know. All we know is she's dead."

"Autopsy?"

"Not yet. The cause of death is obvious, so there's no hurry. Snickersnee." He drew a finger under his own soft jowls.

"With the Norrises' bolo knife?"

"Sure looks like it. The knife was there on the floor, covered with blood."

"How would it get into her room, assuming that Alex Norris didn't take it there?"

"He did, though. He admits it."

"You have a confession?"

"Hell, no. He claims she asked him for it day before yesterday. According to him, she saw him using it to split some kindling, and she said she'd like to have it in her room. He took it to her when he was finished cutting wood. He says."

"Any reason given?"

"She wanted it to protect herself, he says. Santana thinks she was contemplating suicide, but that's what Santana would think, or say he thinks."

"What do fingerprints say, or is that a secret?"

He lit a cigar without offering me one: I voted in Los Angeles. "It's no secret. Both hers and his are on it. Mostly hers."

"That's consistent with suicide."

"It's also consistent with murder. Suicides don't cut themselves that deep, unless they're completely nutty, and she wasn't. Besides, there are no hesitation marks. And the boy admits they quarreled. The D.A. wants him arraigned." He sounded faintly regretful.

"You don't think he did it, though."

"I'll let a jury form my opinion for me. The evidence warrants arraignment, you can see that. Somebody killed her, and the Norris kid was the one that quarreled with her." He switched off the light, and his cigar winked at me like a red eye.

"What about?"

"He won't say. He admits that they quarreled yesterday, that's all."

"Is that what he meant when he said he was responsible?"

"You figure it out." He covered Lucy with the sheet again, and we went outside.

I drove to Mrs. Norris's address. The street was on the precarious edge of the slums, in but not quite of the unofficial ghetto. A street of small well-kept houses standing among neat pocket-handkerchief lawns and flowery borders. Mrs. Norris's white clapboard bungalow was one of the best in its block. There was a postwar Cadillac at the curb in front of it, being admired by a group of Negro children. I parked behind the Cadillac.

Its owner was inside with Mrs. Norris. He was a slight, sallow Mexican in his fifties, with a dry laconic voice and effusive manners. He embraced me with one arm and shook my hand with the other. "Glad to see you, Mr. Archer. Glad you could make it." His breath, which was not unpleasant, smelt of spices. A mummy might look and smell and sound as Santana did, if it started to breathe again in a sudden onrush of enthusiasm.

I drew away, and sat in the armchair Mrs. Norris indicated. "What's the word on your client?"

"They still *habent* the *corpus*. I just passed a bad hour arguing with Judge Bronson. He won't issue a writ. They're going to arraign Alex in Justice Court." He took out a gold cigarette holder, caught Mrs. Norris's look of disapproval, and put it away again, gracefully.

"Can they make it stick?"

He shot a lizard glance at the boy's mother, and shrugged. "I'd feel a little more certain that it won't if we could present a reasonable alternative, you know? I thought suicide, but I don't know if it's tenable."

"I'm afraid not. You've seen the wound?"

"Yes," he said. "Guillotine."

Mrs. Norris shuddered audibly. She was leaning forward in a rocker with her forearms on her knees, her eyes like dark weights in her head. On the wall behind her a Sunday School motto stated that Christ was a silent listener at every conversation.

"Mrs. Norris," I said, "if I could have a look at Lucy's things —"

She straightened. "The police sealed up her room, inside and outside. I can't get in myself, even to clean it up."

"You can," I told Santana.

"Yes. I'll need an order."

"Isn't there anything of hers in the rest of the house?"

Mrs. Norris rose ponderously. "She mostly stayed in her room, but I'll have a look."

As soon as she was gone, Santana moved with short quick steps across the threadbare carpet, and laid a hand on my shoulder. "I didn't like to speak out in front of her. I talked to Alex this morning, and there was another man. Alex saw him go in by Lucy's private entrance Tuesday night, night before last. That's what their fight was about yesterday. He accused her of being a prostitute. Then when he found her dead, he thought he'd forced her to suicide." He removed his weight from my shoulder and spread his hands. "Poor boy."

"Poor girl. Was she one?"

"Not here. Not in Mrs. Norris's house. That one is a highly moral woman."

"No doubt." But there was doubt in my mind about Lucy and her orange silk pyjamas. "Could he give you a description of the man?"

"A very good description." He took out a small leather notebook and opened it. "He was a white man. Curly black hair and Latin features, more Italian than Spanish. Broad-shouldered, above medium height. Light tan tweed jacket, light gabardine trousers. Two-tone sport shoes, brown and white. Dark red tie. General effect that of a prosperous thug. Discount that last though. Alex hated the man on sight, for obvious reasons."

"You've told the police about this?"

"Alex wouldn't let me. He made me swear I wouldn't. The boy's a poetry-reader, Mr. Archer. He would rather die than cast aspersions publicly on her memory. I'm going to tell them anyway, of course, now that I've told you first. Quite soon now. But it would be so much more effective if we could present the man along with the story."

"So I'm to pluck him out of the air. This state is lousy with prosperous thugs. Latin and non-Latin."

"Is it not?" He scurried back to the mohair chesterfield. "But there is your problem."

Mrs. Norris returned, laden with meager booty. A woman's hat and coat. "These were hers. She kept them in the hall closet." Toothbrush and toothpaste, a bottle of mouthwash, one of hair oil, assorted cosmetics. "She had her own little cabinet in the bathroom. Oh, and this."

She handed me a clinical thermometer. I turned it over and found the mercury column. It registered a temperature of 107. I showed it to Santana. "Lucy was really sick, apparently."

"She didn't die of a fever," he said.

Mrs. Norris examined the thermometer. "I don't believe she was running a temperature like that. She wouldn't have been able to walk around. What did Dr. Benning say about her?"

"That she had nothing serious the matter."

"Benning?" Santana said. "Was she Benning's patient?"

"Not exactly. She went to see him once."

"Most people do," he said dryly.

"Let's look at the other things."

The items from the bathroom cabinet could have been bought in any city or town in the United States. There was no druggists's prescription, nothing that could be pinned down to a definite place or person. The coat was equally anonymous. It was a plain black cloth coat, bearing the label of a New York maker who turned out thousands of cheap coats every year.

I was a little surprised by the hat. It was a soft turban made of black wool yarn interwoven with threads of gold. It was simple enough, but something about its shape suggested money.

"With your permission," I said, "I'm going to take this along with me. You're sure there's nothing else of hers around, outside of the room?"

"I don't believe so."

"Who's the best milliner in town?"

"Helen," Santana answered, so quickly that he almost blushed about it. "Her shop is on the Plaza."

Helen's was one of those shops with a single hat in the window, like a masterpiece of plastic art in a gallery. Helen herself was almost a work of art, a small dark middle-aged woman who tripped towards me like an aging ballet dancer.

"You are looking for a gift, perhaps?" Her painted mask-like face formed a slight waiting smile.

"Not exactly. In fact, not at all." I took the black-and-gold turban out of my jacket pocket and handed it to her. "You wouldn't know where this came from?"

Her curved scarlet talons poked and pulled at the hat. "Why?"

"I'm a detective. A woman was killed. This belonged to her."

"Wealth?" She turned it inside out.

"I hardly think so. It's a good hat, though, isn't it?"

"Very good. French workmanship, I do believe."

"You couldn't hazard a guess as to the maker?"

"A guess, perhaps. It has Augustin lines. The way it's folded, you know?" She plucked at the material.

"Where is Augustin?"

"Paris." She pulled the hat on suddenly, struck a pose in front of a mirror on the wall. "Pretty, but not for me. It was made for a blonde. Was your killed woman a blonde?"

"No."

"Then she had bad taste." She removed the hat and gave it back to me. "Augustin has a Los Angeles outlet, you know. Bertha Mackay on Wilshire. Might that help?"

I drove to Los Angeles. Bertha Mackay's hat shop had the hushed solemnity of a funeral chapel. A few handmaidens lazed about in the theatrical light, and paid no attention to me. Tea was being served from a silver service in the rear of the shop. I couldn't imagine Lucy coming here to buy a hat.

A stout woman with blonde coroneted braids was pouring for a bevy of spectacularly hatted females. I addressed her: "May I speak to Miss Mackay?"

"You have that privilege and pleasure." Her smile conveyed the idea that the hat shop and the tea-pouring were charades, good fun but not to be taken seriously.

"Privately, if possible."

"I'm rather busy just now —"

"It won't take a minute."

She removed her hand from the teapot and rose sighing. "Now what?" She led me into a corner.

I had a story ready, which omitted the alarming fact of murder: "I sell cars. A young lady came into the showroom this morning, and asked to try out a new convertible. She went away without leaving her name or address, and left her hat in the car. I'd like to return it to her."

"And sell her a car?"

"If I can. But the hat is worth money, isn't it?" I showed it to her.

She looked up sharply. "How did you know I sold it?"

"A woman who knows hats said it was an Augustin, and that you handled them."

"It *is* worth money. Two hundred dollars, to be exact. I'm not excessively wild about the notion of giving out a customer's name, though. You know all you want to do is sell her a car."

"You sold her a hat."

She smiled, but she was suspicious of me. "What did she look like?"

I took a chance: "She was blonde, a well-groomed blonde."

She didn't deny it. Glancing impatiently towards the tea-party, where the spectacular hats were twittering like birds, she said: "Oh hell, it was Fern Dee bought it. Only don't tell her I told you, she might object. Say you went to a fortune-teller, um?"

"Fern Dee. Where does she live?"

"I haven't the faintest idea. I only saw her the one time, last spring. She saw this hat in the window and walked in and paid cash for it and walked out. I recognized her from her pictures."

"Her pictures?"

"In the newspaper. Don't you read the newspapers? I really must go now." Brusquely, she turned away.

I took my sense of frustration to Morris Cramm. Bach on a harpsichord rustled and clanged behind the door of his walkup apartment. He came to the door softly in stocking feet, and waved me in without uttering a word. When the side was finished, he switched the Capehart off and said, "Hello there, Lew."

The Capehart was the only valuable thing in the dingy room, apart from Morris's filing-cabinet brain. He was the nightspot legman for a Hollywood columnist, a small middle-aging man with thick glasses and the inability to forget a fact.

"I need a small transfusion of information."

"You know my terms. Eye for eye, tooth for tooth, money for information. The Mosaic law won't let me turn off good music for nothing."

"I'm on the side of the angels this time. You should take that into account. I'm trying to clear a Negro boy of a pending murder charge. I don't even know if I'll be paid."

"You'll be paid. *Moi aussi.*"

I screwed up a five-dollar bill and tossed it to him. "Money-grubber."

"Scavenger. Go ahead."

"I want to talk to a woman. Name is Fern Dee. You've

heard of her, probably. Everyone else has."

"Except you, eh? She Superchiefed from Chicago last year with Angel Durano. I saw them on the Strip every night for a while. I don't know where or what she came up out of. Claimed to be a dancer, but he backed her in a revue and she flopped, dismally. Do you still want to talk to her?"

"Very much."

"You know who Durano is, don't you? The name for him back east is the Enforcer. When the Syndicate got tired of playing footsie with Mickey, they sent Durano out to finish him. In a business way, you understand. Nothing violent, unless it becomes essential." He took off his spectacles and wiped them. "Charming place and time we live in. Charming people."

"Where are these particular charming people?"

"I haven't seen them lately. Durano has himself a place in the desert, and they could be living there, though it's hardly the season. They could be back in Chicago, but I doubt it. Durano is running this territory permanently." He clicked his teeth. "That's a nice fat five dollar's worth."

"It's pretty hot in the desert this time of year."

"Heat doesn't seem to bother Durano. He's got ice water in his veins. I saw him in the Springs in the middle of August. It was close to 110 in the shade, and he was wearing a top-coat."

"Is that where his place is — Palm Springs?"

"It's a few miles beyond Palm Springs, towards Indio. Everybody out there knows him. Better be nice to him, Lew, if you get that far. He was indicted for homicide once, even in Chicago."

I said that I was always nice to people. The harpsichord drowned me out.

$X \; X \; X$

The sun was low when I reached Palm Springs, glowing

dull red like a cigar-butt balanced on the rim of the horizon. The tall sky rose above it, blue-grey like a column of smoke. Beyond the town, which was miniatured by space, the chameleon desert burned red in the sun's reflection. It was hot.

I stopped at a highway gas-station and ordered a tankful. Paying the attendant, I mentioned casually that Mr. Durano had invited me to dinner.

"Mr. Angelo Durano?"

"That's the one. Know him?"

His manner changed perceptibly, became a little contemptuous and a little obsequious. "I don't know him, no. He bought some gas here once, at least his chauffeur did. He was in the car." He eyed me curiously.

"It's a lovely doll he travels with," I said. "You see her, too? The blonde?"

"I didn't see her. Here's your change, sir."

"Keep it. You don't know where he lives, do you? They gave me full instructions how to find it, but this is new country to me."

"Sure, sir. He lives on Canyon Road. Take the second turn to the right and you can't miss it. It's a great big place with round towers. Used to be a gambling casino in the old days."

It stood by itself on a slight rise like somebody's idea of a castle in Spain. The last rays of the sun washed its stucco walls in purple light. Its acreage was surrounded by an eight-foot wire fence, barbed along the top. The single gate was closed and guarded.

The guard wore riding breeches, a Stetson, and a suede windbreaker bulky enough to hide a gun. When I stopped in front of the gate, he waved me on. I got out and approached him. "Is this Durano's place?"

"Beat it, mac. This is private property."

"I didn't think it was a national park. I'm looking for Mr.

Durano."

"Keep right on looking." He took a step towards me, left foot first, right foot coming up behind. In the shadow of his hat, his face was thick with scar-tissue. "Someplace else."

I spoke soothingly: "Why don't you ask Mr. Durano if he'll see me? My name is Lew Archer."

"Mr. Durano ain't here. Now amscray, mac. I mean it." He acted out his meaning, advancing his left shoulder and balling his right fist.

"Miss Dee, then. Fern Dee. Can I talk to her?"

The name had an effect on him, interrupting his preparations to hit me. "You know Miss Dee?"

"I have something of hers." I reached for the turban.

"Keep your hands away from your pockets." He moved up close to me and patted me down, then jerked the hat out of my jacket pocket. "Where did you get ahold of this?"

"I'll tell Miss Dee."

"That's what you think," he said in brilliant repartee. "You better come on inside."

The man who guarded the front door relieved him at the gate. Durano received me in the great hall. It was a large rectangular room with a high roof supported by black oak beams, crowded with stiff old Spanish furniture, carpeted with Oriental rugs. A baronial room, built for giants.

Durano was a tired-looking little man. He might have been a moderately successful grocer or barkeep who had come to California for his health. Clearly his health was poor. Even in the stifling heat of the room he looked pale and chilly, as if he had caught a slight case of chronic death from one of his victims.

He had been playing solitaire on one end of a refectory table. He rose and advanced towards me, his legs shuffling feebly in wrinkled blue trousers that bagged at the knees. The upper part of his body was swathed in a heavy turtleneck sweater. He had two days' beard on his chin, like motheaten grey plush.

"Mr. Durano?" I said. "My name is Lew Archer."

The guard spoke up behind me: "He brung this little hat with him, Mr. Durano. Said it belongs to Fern — Miss Dee."

Durano took the hat from him, and turned it over in his blue hands. His eyes were like thin stab-wounds filled with watery blood. "Where did you get this, Mr. Archer?"

"I sort of thought I'd like to tell the owner where I got it."

"You sort of thought." He smiled at me quite pleasantly, and pressed his toe into the center of the rug that he was standing on. Two more men entered the room.

Durano nodded to the guard behind me, who reached to pin my arms. I turned on him, landed one punch, and took a very hard counter in the neck. One of the men behind me hit my kidneys like a heavy truck-bumper. I turned on him and kneed him, catching his companion with an elbow under the chin. The original guard delivered a rabbit-punch that made my head ring like a gong. Under that clangor, Durano was saying quietly:

"Where did you get the hat?"

I didn't say. The two men held me upright by the arms while the guard employed my face and body as punching bags. At intervals Durano asked me politely to tell him about the hat. After a while he shook his head. My handlers deposited me in a chair which swung on a wire from the ceiling in great circles. It swung out over the desert into black space.

When I came to, a young man was standing over me. He had curly black hair, Mediterranean features and coloring, light tan jacket, red tie. Alex's description had been excellent. There was an empty water-glass in his hand, and my face was dripping.

"Did you get the hat from Lucy?" he said.

"Lucy?" My mouth was numb, and I lisped. "I don't know

any Lucy."

"Sure you do." He shattered the glass on the arm of my chair, and held the jagged base up close to my eyes. "You tell me all about it like a nice fella."

"Nix, Gino," the old man said. "I got a better idea as usual."

They conferred in low voices, and the younger man left the room. He returned with a photograph in a silver frame, which he held in front of my face. It was a studio portrait, of the kind intended for use as publicity cheesecake. Against a black velvet background, a young blonde half-reclined in a gossamer sort of robe that was split to show one bent leg. Though she was adequately stacked and pretty in a rather dull, corn-fed way, her best feature was her long pull-taffy hair. The picture was signed in a childish hand: "To my Angel, with love and everything. Fern."

"You know the dame?" Gino demanded. "Ever seen her before?"

I thought I had, and said I hadn't.

"You're sure?" The shard of glass was still in his other hand.

"I see a lot of blondes. How can I be sure?"

"Where did you get the hat, then?"

"I won it in a raffle."

Gino's face thickened, and his eyes almost crossed. Durano stepped in front of him. "Leave him alone, leave him go. There is heat on, remember. We keep our hands clean." He scoured his thin blue hands with each other. They sounded like sticks rubbing together.

Gino backed away, joining the three others who stood in a semi-circle behind Durano. The old man leaned towards me:

"Mr. Detective, I don't know who you work for, I don't care. You took a nice good look at the lady in the picture? You ever see her, come back and visit me. I promise a nicer reception."

I turned my face away from his charnel-house breath.

At midnight I was back in Santa Teresa, knocking on the door of Santana's house. He came to the door in a red velvet smoking-jacket, a volume of the Holmes-Pollock letters open under his arm.

"What under heaven?" he said in Spanish. "Your face, Mr. Archer!"

"I had a little plastic surgery done."

"Come in. Let me get you a drink."

Over the drink, Scotch and water in equal proportions, I told him where I had gone on the trail of the hat, and what had happened there.

"Where is the hat now?"

"Durano kept it. After all, he probably paid for it."

"And what do you make of it all?" Santana hunched his shoulders and spread his hands palms upward on his knees. In his paneled library, surrounded by books, he resembled an old spider at the center of his web.

"There isn't too much to go on, certainly not enough to try and have Durano and his torpedo brought in. That would take powerful medicine."

"I agree."

"What there is adds up to the reasonable alternative you asked for. Fern Dee was Durano's girl friend. She got fed up with him and the desert, as anybody but a gila monster would, and she left him. But that's one of the things the executives of the Syndicate can't permit, this year especially. Their women learn too much about their sources of income, ever to be allowed to run out on them. Besides, Durano is old and ugly and sick. She took her life in her hands when she left him, and she must have known it." I sipped my drink. The whisky burned my lips where they had been cut.

"And Lucy?"

"See how this sounds to you. Lucy was Fern Dee's maid, probably her confidante. She knew where Fern Dee had gone, perhaps she had instructions to follow her when she got the chance, and bring her clothes —"

"To Santa Teresa here."

"Evidently. Fern let her keep some of the clothes, and gave her money to live on quietly. There could have been blackmail involved, but I doubt that."

"Blackmail seems to be indicated," the lawyer said.

"It's doubtful. Gino traced Lucy down, don't forget. He talked to her in her room Tuesday night, and she didn't tell him where Fern was."

"You think that is why she was killed, that this Gino killed her?"

"It's a reasonable alternative," I said. "In any case, your client was an innocent bystander. He stood too near the fire, and got burned."

"We still have the task of proving it. Can we question this Gino in any way? Where is he?"

"In Santa Teresa," I said. "He followed me out of Palm Springs in a Buick. It was a pretty crude tail-job, and I lost him on 99. But he should be in town by now. He'll be looking for me. Durano thinks I can lead him to Fern Dee."

"Can you?"

"I think so."

"Do you have a gun?"

I patted my pocket. "I keep it in the glove compartment of my car."

Santana stood up. "I believe that I had better call the police."

"No," I said. "You want to give them the man along with the story."

"A doctor, at least. Those are nasty cuts on your mouth. They need attention."

"I'm on my way to see a doctor — Dr. Benning."

Santana exploded, dryly, like a puff-ball. "He is a bum physician, Mr. Archer. A charlatan. Only those who can find nothing better go to Benning. Those who have to."

"Girls that get caught, for example?"

"That is the rumor. As a matter of fact, I can confirm the rumor. I have many sorts of clients."

"I'm not proud."

There were lights on both the first and second stories of Dr. Benning's house. I parked at the curb and looked up and down the street. Yellow traffic lights winked on the bare asphalt. The sidewalks were deserted. A few late cars rolled into sight and out of mind. There was no sign of Gino's four-hole Buick sedan.

I pushed the bell-button under the large shabby sign. I heard quiet footsteps in the hallway, and Benning's long face was framed in the dirty glass pane. The light came on over my head. Benning unlocked the door, and opened it cautiously. His pale eyeballs were bloodshot, but not from sleep. He was fully clothed, in the suit I had seen him in that morning.

I got the curious idea that Dr. Benning had been crying.

His speech was slightly thick: "Archer, isn't it? You've been hurt, man."

"That can wait."

I leaned my shoulder against the half-open door, and he stepped back to let me enter. Under the lamp in the hallway, his bald pink pate looked innocent and vulnerable like a baby's. He took his worn felt hat from a brass rack on the wall, and placed it on his head.

"Going somewhere?"

The gesture had been unconscious. He didn't understand me. "No, I'm not going anywhere." His tone implied that he never had, had never even expected to. He moved back against the wall, out of the grim light. Beyond his dwarf shadow a flight of stairs rose into darkness.

"I came across a funny thing this afternoon, Dr. Benning. Your patient Lucy Deschamps — your ex-patient — had a clinical thermometer. Mrs. Norris found it in her bathroom."

"What's funny about that? Most people do, particularly hypochondriacs."

"The funny thing was that it registered a temperature of 107."

"Good lord, man. That's usually fatal in adults. Was she so ill as that? I had no idea." His reaction was phony.

He lifted his hat with his left hand and began to polish the top of his head with his right palm. It was ludicrous. I didn't know whether to laugh at him or weep with him.

"I don't think she was ill at all, or had a temperature. The weather did it."

He blinked at me, still polishing his scalp. Futility and unease surrounded him like an odor. "It's never been that hot in Santa Teresa."

"Lucy came from Palm Springs last August 16. It was that hot in Palm Springs in the middle of August."

"She told me San Francisco," he said feebly.

"Maybe she did. If you talked to her at all. Which I doubt."

"You're calling me a liar?" His body stayed loose against the wall, unstiffened by anger or pride.

Somewhere upstairs, above our heads, there was a scraping sound, a small flurry of movement. Then he stiffened.

"You are a liar," I said. "You said that Lucy was a hypochondriac, that fear might have motivated her suicide. But she hadn't taken her temperature in a month. A hypochondriac takes it every day."

"I may have misjudged her. I probably did. People make mistakes."

"No. She didn't even come here to see you. She came to see your receptionist. You lied this morning to cover up for Miss Tennent."

"I had to —" He broke off sharply, jammed the hat on his head, huddled long and thin against the wall.

"I want to speak to Miss Tennent. Is she upstairs?"

"No. I don't know where she is. She's gone away."

"I'll have a look, if you don't mind."

"No!" He moved sideways to the foot of the stairs. His actions had lost all sense of style or timing. Something had beaten the last vestiges of pride out of his body.

"Even if you do mind."

I pushed him to one side and went up. A dingy hallway lined with doors ran the length of the second story. A yellow tape of light showed under one of the doors. I opened it quietly.

The woman who had called herself Miss Tennent was packing a suitcase on an unmade bed on the far side of the room. She was leaning over the bed with her narrow back to me, the short black hair falling about her face.

She spoke without turning:

"You needn't come crawling back, Sam. I'm taking off, and you know it. Make it a clean break."

I said nothing. She turned sideways, still not looking at me, and picked up a bottle of black liquid that might have been hair dye. Wrapping it in a black brassiere, she pushed it into the suitcase.

She went on talking in a toneless voice, the words dropping cold and heavy from her hidden mouth. "Lucy and I were like sisters, you know that? All these years, since the South Side, she was my one true friend. So you killed her, Sam. All right. Lucy's finished. So are we. Anything you did for me when I needed doing for, you canceled it out. Just take it like a man, that's all I'm asking. Nobody's turning you in."

Behind and below me, Benning was laboring up the stairs. I had pushed him pretty hard. His breathing was audible, to the woman as well as me.

"Sam?" she cried on a rising note, and whirled in a dancer's movement.

I moved towards her. She reached backwards into the suitcase for something. I took her by the wrists. Her body was made of whalebone covered with plush. It was hard to subdue.

"Easy, Fern," I said. "I wouldn't hurt you."

Downstairs, in the front of the house, the doorbell rang. The woman started. We stood together by the half-packed suitcase, the unmade bed, breathing hard into each other's faces.

"If I turn you loose, will you promise not to shoot me?"

"I promise nothing."

I lifted her from behind and carried her into the hallway. Below, the front door opened.

"Dr. Benning?" It was Gino's voice.

"Don't let him in," I shouted.

Benning never heard me. A submachine gun pounded like an air-hammer at the shaky walls of his house.

The woman had ceased struggling in my arms. She was stiff with terror. I swung her behind me, took my revolver out, steadied my gun arm on the newel post. Gino came to the foot of the stairs with the Thompson in his hands. I shot him carefully through the face. Then I went to the telephone.

When I returned to the hallway, Benning was lying near the open door, his head in the woman's lap. His hat was on its side beside him, in a growing pool of blood. When he spoke, the words made bubbling sounds in his throat:

"You won't leave me, Fern? You promised you'd never leave me. I did it for you, everything for you."

"I won't leave you. Crazy fool. Crazy man."

She cradled the naked, vulnerable head in her hands. He sighed, and his life came out bright-colored at the mouth. It was Dr. Benning who departed.

Sitting against the wall with the dead man in her arms, she talked to me, in the same cold heavy voice:

"I'm a swell picker, aren't I? Durano, and now Sam Benning. I heard about Sam from a girl friend in the Springs, when I was two months gone. I could stand a trick baby, but not Durano's. Did you ever see Durano?"

"I've seen him." I sat on the bottom step and offered her a cigarette, which she refused.

"I stomached Angel for two years and a half. I owed him about that long. He took me out of a strip joint in Gary and gave me everything. Everything I wanted. But a baby was too much. I took a runout powder, and came up here to Sam. He didn't know me from Eve, but he took care of me. Even when he found out who I was, and who Durano was, he let me stay. He wanted me to stay. He was crazy about me, crazy in more ways than one. But he had guts." She looked down at the blind face clasped to her breast: "You weren't afraid, were you, Sammy? Not for a while, anyway."

Her gaze, blue and remote, swung back to me: "He started to lose his grip when Lucy came. She was my maid, sort of, I brought her out of Gary along with me. Hell, she was my best friend. Too bad Sammy never got that straight. Lucy came up last month and brought my things, all she could get away with. Then she was afraid to go back. I didn't want her to, either. Durano would squeeze it out of her where I was. So Sam found her a place to stay up here. I knew it couldn't last after Lucy came. A month was the best we could hope for. Durano's men found Lucy then. She didn't cover her traces the way I did. Gino went to see her Tuesday night. She had to play along. What could she do? She said she needed forty-eight hours to finger me, that I was hiding out in the mountains and only came to town once a week for groceries.

"They left a watch on her. It took her most of yesterday to throw them off and get over here without giving me away. I wasn't even here when she arrived. But Sam was. She spilled the thing to him, and he got the fantods and decided that Lucy had to be silenced. He knew that if she talked to Gino, that was the end of us. Sam was afraid for his life, but mostly I guess he didn't want to lose me. So he sneaked over there in the middle of the night and cut her throat for her. Today after you came I asked him if he did it and he admitted it. You had good reason to be afraid, didn't you, Sammy?" A dark and cynical tenderness growled in her voice. "Stop me if I'm breaking your heart, Archer or whatever your name is."

Somewhere outside in the night a siren screamed, very loud, as if the noise could make up for its tardiness.

"They'll be holding you for material witness," I said. "At least."

She shrugged, and the dead face moved against her. "I couldn't care less. Where would I want to go that I haven't been? Anyway, Angel can't get at me in the clink."

She was still in the same position when the city police walked in. She looked up at them coldly.

They held me, too, until Santana established that I had shot Gino in self-defense. I was in the Sheriff's office when Alex Norris was released. His mother was there with Santana, waiting to greet him. It was bright morning by then.

Alex had very little to say to his mother. He wanted to know where Lucy's body was. When Santana told him, he set out for the morgue by himself. I felt sorry for Mrs. Norris, but there was nothing I could do for her. Her son had stood too close to the fire and been burned. Chicago, the northern cities, had caught up with both of them.

Gino died in the County Hospital two days later, without

having had a visitor. His automobile was charged with con-
cealment of weapons, found guilty, and impounded for official
use by the Sheriff's staff. Fern Dee, or whatever her name
was, was released the following Monday. She disappeared. At
the end of the month, Santana sent me a check for eighty
dollars. One day's pay and expenses.

# THE ANGRY MAN

# THE ANGRY MAN

## Preface by Tom Nolan

Written in the middle 1950s, "The Angry Man" shows Ross Macdonald working with great assurance: a pro-and-a-half by now, and on the brink of even better things.

The first sentence pulls the reader immediately into Archer's narrative, and into his would-be client's nightmare. Throughout the text, the writer's technique is deft, his humor nicely wry, his symbolism striking.

Note thwarted Jerry, who neglects his pretty Zinnia to cultivate inhuman blossoms — only to end sprawled amongst those blooms, "a fine funeral display."

Note the contrast between the psychiatric social worker (Mr. Parish, a secular priest) in his shabby office, helping the needy and the truly sick ("my family") — and the Beverly Hills psychiatrist in his glossy quarters, catering to the neuroses of the idle rich.

Note the artful foreshadowings ("I can't turn the police on him ... They'd shoot him down like a dog") that are also psychological clues, and that make second readings of Macdonald works uniquely rewarding.

Nelson Algren was an author important to Millar/Macdonald in the 1940s and '50s. *The Ivory Grin* (built from "Strangers in Town") was written under the influence of Algren works like *The Man with the Golden Arm*. The penultimate paragraph of "The Angry Man" may sound an echo of an Algren short story Ken Millar much admired, one where the hapless victim insists he was only going out to buy "A Bottle of Milk for Mother."

In "The Angry Man," Archer learns from Mr. Parish a little

about how to see beyond a simplistic, good-and-bad worldview. In *The Doomsters* (which grew from this novelette), the detective — propelled by events in the author's own life — would learn a good deal more.

*The Doomsters* would prove a milestone on the road of Ross Macdonald's mature vision, a road he was already well along when he penned "The Angry Man."

Looking back in 1976 on the life of the fictional private eye who first came to the page pseudonymously as Joe Rogers in 1945, Ross Macdonald judged: "Archer just wasn't as well done as Spade or Marlowe. It took him a while to develop into anything substantial. The real change in him, I think, occurred in *The Doomsters*; he became a man who was not so much trying to find the criminal as understand him. He became more of a representative of man rather than just a detective who finds things out."

## NOTE

" 'Archer just wasn't as well done' ": Clifford A. Ridley, "Yes, Most of My Chronicles Are Chronicles of Misfortune," *National Observer*, July 31, 1976.

# THE ANGRY MAN

I thought at first sheer terror was his trouble. He shut the door of my office behind him and stood against it, panting like a dog. He was a gaunt man in blue jeans almost black with sweat and dirt. Short rust-colored hair grew like stubble on his hatless scalp. His face was still young, but it had been furrowed by pain and clawed by anger.

"They're after me. I need help." The words came from deep in his laboring chest. "You're a detective, aren't you?"

"A sort of one. Sit down and take a little time to get your breath. You shouldn't run up those stairs."

He laughed. It was an ugly strangled sound, like water running down a drain. "I've been running all night. All night."

Warily, he circled the chair in front of my desk. He lifted the chair in a sudden movement and set it back to front against the wall and straddled it. His shoulders were wide enough to yoke a pair of oxen. His hands gripped the back of the chair and his chin came down and rested between them while he watched me. His eyes were narrow and blue, brilliant with suspicion.

"Running from what?" I said.

"From them." He looked at the closed door, then over his shoulder at the blank wall. "They're after me, I tell you."

"That makes twice you've told me. It isn't what I'd call a detailed story."

"It's no story." He leaned forward, tilting the chair. "It's true. There's nothing they wouldn't do, or haven't done."

"Who are they?"

"The same ones. It's always the same ones. The cheats. The liars. The people who run things." He went into singsong: "The ones that locked me up and threw the key away. They'll do it again if they can. You've got to help me."

He was beginning to disturb me badly. "Why do I have to help you?"

"Because I say so." He bit his lip. "I mean, who else can I go to? Who else is there?"

"You could try the police."

He spat. "They're in on the deal. Don't talk police to me, or doctors or lawyers or any of the others that sold me out. I want somebody working for me, on my side. If it's money you're worried about, there's plenty of money in it. I'll be rolling in money when I get my rights. Rolling in it, I tell you."

"Uh-huh."

He sprang to his feet, striking the wall a back-handed blow which left a dent in the plaster. His chair toppled. "Don't you believe me? It's the truth I'm telling you. I'm damn near a millionaire if I had my rights."

He started to pace, up and down in front of my desk, his swivelling blue eyes always watching me. I said:

"Pick up that chair."

"I'm giving the orders. For a change."

"Pick up the chair and sit in it," I said.

He stood still for a long moment, his face changing. Dull sorrow filmed his eyes like transparent lacquer. "I'm sorry. I didn't mean to fly off the handle. It's just when I think about *them*."

"The chair," I said.

He stooped and picked it up and sat in it. "I'm sorry, Mr. Archer."

"I'm not Archer," I lied. "You've got me wrong."

His eyes blazed wide. "Who are you then? Archer's the name on the door."

"I keep Mr. Archer's books, answer his telephone for him. Why didn't you say you wanted Mr. Archer?"

"I thought that you were him," he answered dully. "A friend of mine, back where I came from, told me if I ever sprung myself

— if I ever got here to L.A., that Mr. Archer would give me a fair throw if anybody would. Where is he?"

I countered with a question: "What's your friend's name?"

"He has no name. I mean I don't remember."

"Where did you spring yourself from?"

"It was a slip of the tongue. I didn't say that. Anyway, what business is it of yours? You're not Mr. Archer."

"Folsom? San Quentin?"

He was silent, his face like stone. After a while he said: "I'll talk to Mr. Archer."

"I'll call him for you." I reached for the telephone and started to dial a number. "Who shall I say wants him?"

"No you don't." His stormy mind had flashes of intuition. "I know what you're up to, ringing in the cops." He leaped across the desk and tore the phone from my hands. "And you *are* Mr. Archer, aren't you? You're a liar, too, like the rest of them. I come here looking for a fair throw and I get the same old dirty deal again. You're one of *them*, aren't you?"

I said: "Put the telephone back on the desk and sit down."

"To hell with you. You can't scare me. One thing, when a man goes through what I've been through, I'm not afraid any more. You hear me?" His voice was rising.

"They hear you in Glendale. Sit down and be quiet now."

He threw the telephone at my head. I ducked. The telephone crashed through the window and hung there on its wire. I reached for the upper righthand drawer of my desk, the one that contained the automatic. But he forestalled me.

"No you don't," he said.

His hand went into his pocket and came out holding a gun. It was a .32 Smith and Wesson revolver, nickel-plated. It wasn't much of a gun, but it was enough to freeze me where I stood.

"Put your hands up," he said. "Give me your word that you won't call the police."

"I can give it. It won't be worth anything."

"That's what I thought. You're a liar like the rest. Get away from that desk."

"Make me. You're crazy if you think —"

He let out a yelp of fury. "I am not crazy."

He dropped the little revolver and reached for me. His hooked hands swung together and clamped on my throat. He dragged me bodily across the desk. He was tremendously strong. His pectorals were massively sculptured under the wet blue shirt. His eyes were closed. They had long reddish lashes like a girl's. He looked almost serene. Then water sprang out in little rows of droplets across his forehead. His iron fingers tightened on my throat, and daylight began to wane.

His face opened suddenly, eyes and mouth, as if he had wakened out of a walking nightmare. The blue eyes were bewildered, the mouth pulled wry by remorse. "I'm sorry. You hate me now. You'll never help me now."

His hands dropped to his sides and hung useless there. Relieved of their support, I went to my knees. Bright-speckled darkness rushed through my head like a wind. When its roaring subsided and I got to my feet, he was gone. So was the bright revolver.

I pulled myself to my feet and dragged the telephone in through the broken window. It still had a dial tone, not quite as loud as the singing tone in my head. I dialed a police number. The desk-sergeant's voice focused my wits, and I hung up without saying a word.

A homicidal maniac, or reasonable facsimile of one, had taken me in my own office. That would be a pretty story for the papers, good advertising for a private detective. Clients would be lining up six deep at my door. I sat and looked at the telephone, trying to decide whether to throw it out the window permanently.

There were footsteps in the outer office, too rapid and light for a man's. As I crossed the room, they paused outside my door. I pulled it open. A woman in a dark suit stumbled in, attached to the knob. Her jet black ducktail bob was slightly disarrayed. She was breathless.

"Are you Mr. Archer?"

I looked her over and decided that there was no harm in admitting it.

She swayed towards me, wafting in springtime odors from the young slopes of her body. "I'm so glad you're all right, that I got here first."

"First before what?"

"Before Carl. He came to Dr. Grantland's office — where I work — and said that he was on his way to see you. He demanded money to pay you with. I went back to get the doctor, to see if he could reason with him. As soon as my back was turned, Carl rifled the petty cash drawer in the desk."

"Who is Carl?"

"My husband. Please forgive me, I'm not making much sense, am I?" Her dark blue glance slid over my shoulder and rested on the jagged hole in the window. "Has Carl been here already?"

"Something was. A man on a cyclone."

"A big young man in working clothes? With short blond hair?"

I nodded.

"And he was violent." It wasn't a question. It was a leaden statement of despair.

"He started to choke me to death, but he changed his mind. Flighty. Did you say he's your husband?"

"Yes."

"You're not wearing a wedding ring."

"I know I'm not. But we're still man and wife, in the legal sense. Of course I could have had an automatic divorce, after the trouble." She slumped against the doorframe. Her dark enormous eyes and her carmine mouth provided the only color in her face. "I knew it. I knew he was lying. They'd never let him go in his condition. He must have escaped. It's what I've been afraid of." A few sobs racked her. She swallowed them, and straightened.

"Come in and sit down. You need a drink."

"I don't drink."

"Not even water?"

I brought her a paper cupful from the cooler and stood over her chair while she drained it.

"Where did Carl escape from?"

"He's been in the Security Hospital in Mendocino for nearly five years." She crumpled the cup in her hands, and twisted it. "It's a state institution for the criminally insane, in case you don't know."

"I do know. Is he that bad?"

"As bad as possible," she said to the twisted cup. "Carl killed his father, you see. He was never tried for the murder, he was so obviously — unbalanced. All the psychiatrists agreed, for once. The judge was a friend of the family, and had him committed without a public trial."

"Where did all this happen?"

"In the Valley, in Citrus Junction. It was a tragic thing for all of us. It happened on Thanksgiving Day, five years ago. Carl was home from Camarillo, and we were having a sort of family reunion."

"Was he a mental patient at the time?"

"He had been, but he was out on leave of absence. We all thought he was on his way to being cured. It was almost a happy day, our first for a long time — until it happened. We should never have left him alone with his father for a minute. I still don't think he meant to kill the old man. He simply went into one of his terrible rages, and when he came out of it old Mr. Heller was dead. Choked to death." Her heavy eyes came up to my face. "I don't know why I'm telling you all this. You have no part in my troubles. Nobody could possibly want a part of them."

It was a hot bright morning, but the draft from the broken

window was cold on the back of my neck. "What brought him to me, I wonder?"

"One of the men he knew in — the institution. Someone you'd helped. He told me that this morning. Carl believes that he's an innocent man, you see. He thinks he's perfectly well, that everyone's been persecuting him unjustly. It's typical of paranoia, according to Dr. Grantland."

"Dr. Grantland is your employer?"

"Yes."

"Does he know Carl?"

"Of course. He treated him for a while before — it happened. Dr. Grantland is a psychiatrist."

"Does he think Carl is dangerous?"

"I'm afraid so. The only one that doesn't is Mr. Parish, and he's not a real psychiatrist."

"What is he?"

"Mr. Parish is a psychiatric social worker, in Citrus Junction. He stood up for Carl when they sent him away, but it didn't do any good." She rose, and fumbled at the clasp of her cheap imitation-leather saddlebag. "I'll be glad to pay you for the window. I'm sorry about this — about poor Carl."

"Poor everybody," I said.

She gave me a bewildered look. "What do you mean, poor everybody?"

"Your husband is carrying a gun."

Her mouth opened. When it finally closed, it was a thin red line. Her eyes focused like a blue spotlight on my face. "How do you know?"

"He was kind enough to show it to me. It looked like a Smith and Wesson .32 revolver."

"Did he threaten you with it?"

"It wasn't a water-pistol, and we weren't playing cowboys and Indians. Does he know how to handle a gun?"

"Carl was a rifleman in the infantry." Her eyes were darkly

luminous like clouds containing lightning. She held out a five-dollar bill to me. "Will this cover the window? It's all the cash I have with me. I have to go."

"Forget the window. We should call the police."

"No." The word broke like a dry sob from her lips. "I can't turn the police on him. You know what they'll do if they catch him and he resists. They'll shoot him down like a dog. I've got to go myself and warn Jerry that he's out."

"Jerry?"

"Jerry Heller, Carl's brother in Citrus Junction. He blames Jerry for everything that's happened to him. I've got to get to Jerry before he does."

"I'll go along."

She looked at me dubiously. "I couldn't afford to pay you very much."

"I don't put a dollar-sign on people's lives. Let's go."

We left her battered Chevrolet in the parking lot of my building, and took my car. Driving out Ventura into the Valley, she told me her name, Mildred Heller, and something about her background.

She had been very young, just out of Hollywood High, when Carl Heller entered her life. It was 1943, and he was a new young private in the Army. They met at a church canteen. She was susceptible, and he was strong and masculine and handsome in a rather strange way of his own. They fell in love and got married, with her parents' reluctant consent, a week before he was shipped out to the Marianes. When she saw him again in 1945, he was in the disturbed ward of a veterans' hospital.

They picked up the pieces together as well as they could. After his discharge, they went to live on his family's lemon ranch. The years of waiting had been hard, but the next few years were harder. Carl and his family didn't get along. His father was crippled with arthritis, and tried to run the ranch from his wheelchair. Carl's older brother Jerry actually ran it.

Carl wouldn't take orders from either of them. And then there was Jerry's wife, who regarded the younger couple as interlopers.

Carl loafed around the house for two years, alternately brooding and raging. Finally he became impossible to live with, and his father had him committed to the state hospital. A year later Carl came home, ate a Thanksgiving dinner, and strangled his father with the rope from the old man's bathrobe. Now Mildred was afraid it was Jerry's turn.

I shifted my eyes from the road to look at her. Huddled in the corner of the seat, she seemed thinner and smaller and older than she had.

"Aren't you afraid of what he'll do to you?"

"No," she said, "I'm not. He's never tried to hurt me, never laid a hand on me. Sometimes I've almost wished he would, and put an end to it. What does my life amount to, after all? I can't even have a child. What have I got to lose?"

"You're a loyal girl, to stick to him."

"Am I? My people don't believe in divorce."

"And you don't either?"

"I don't believe in anything any more. Good or bad."

She turned her face away, and we drove in silence for another hour. The spring color of the hills was like Paris green. Gradually the hills slipped back into hazy distance. The highway ran smooth and straight across the citrus flatlands. Geometrically planted lemon trees stretched out like deep green corduroy around us. At her direction, I left the highway and turned up a county road.

A weatherwarped sign, *Jeremiah Heller Lemons*, marked the entrance to a private lane. It led us through nearly a mile of lemon groves spotted with yellowing fruit. At its end a tile-roofed ranch house sprawled in the sun. When I switched off my engine, the silence was almost absolute.

The house was an old adobe which must have stood for

several generations. Each new generation had added a wing of its own. A station wagon and a dusty jeep were parked on the gravel in front of the garages.

The silence was broken by a screen door's percussion. Mildred jumped in her seat. She was strung as taut as a fiddlestring.

A striking blonde came out on the verandah and stood with her arms folded over her breasts, watching us as we got out of the car. She wore black satin slacks, a white silk shirt, and green enamel earrings in the middle of the day. Her eyes were the color and texture of the earrings.

"Why Mildred. What brings you here? Long time no see. I thought you had a job in Los Angeles, darling. Or did you lose that one, too?"

"I took the day off."

"Well, that's nice, isn't it? Who's the boyfriend?"

"Mr. Archer isn't my boyfriend."

"No? Don't tell me you're still burning a vestal candle for Carl. Isn't that one pretty much of a forlorn hope?"

"Please, Zinnia. Don't." Mildred moved slowly up the verandah steps, as if she had to force herself to approach the blonde woman or enter the area of the house. "I came to tell you about Carl."

"How fascinating. Let's get out of this bloody sun, then, shall we? It plays hell with my complexion."

Her voice was low and dry and monotonous, the voice of a vicious boredom. It affected me like a rattlesnake's buzzing signal. We followed her switching hips into a cavernous living room walled with adobe, roofed with black oak beams. The breeze from a cooling system chilled me, or perhaps it was the blonde. She said:

"What's your poison, Mr. Archer? I've been trying to think of an excuse to have a drink, anyway. I'm Zinnia Heller, by the way, since Milly has forgotten her manners as usual."

I mislaid mine, deliberately. "I'd go easy on her, Mrs. Heller. She came to warn you —"

She turned to Mildred, her thin plucked eyebrows arching. "To warn me, dear? Aren't we getting a little melodramatic?"

"Carl has escaped," the younger woman said. "He hitchhiked to Los Angeles last night and turned up this morning at the office where I work."

"Escaped from Mendocino?"

"Yes. And he's violent, Zinnia. He made some wild threats against Jerry."

"You called the police, I hope." The blonde's low buzzing voice had risen at least an octave.

"Not yet. Mr. Archer here is a private detective. Carl attacked him this morning."

"And you think he's coming here?"

"I know he is. He's always believed that Jerry railroaded him."

"You thought so yourself at one time, if memory serves me."

"I never did, Zinnia, and you know it. All I ever claimed was that I had a right to some of the money, no matter *what* Carl did."

"Well, the law disagreed." Zinnia went to a bar in the corner of the room, poured herself a stiff brown drink from a cut-glass decanter, and gulped it straight. "Speaking of the law, I'd better call Ostervelt about this. Wasn't that the idea?"

"Yes. Of course. The Sheriff knows Carl. He won't hurt him unless he absolutely has to."

Zinnia picked up a portable telephone and sat down with it in her gleaming satin lap. Her sharp red fingertip hesitated in the dial hole. "You're sure all this is true, what you've been telling me? Carl really did escape? You're not just trying to throw a scare into me, for old time's sake?"

I said: "I saw your brother-in-law, Mrs. Heller. He's disturbed, and he's got a gun. You'd better tell the Sheriff about the gun. And your husband should be warned."

"Will do." She had recovered her composure. She talked to the duty deputy like a brigadier giving orders to a lieutenant colonel. I was once a lieutenant colonel, and I knew.

"Where is your husband?" I said when she put down the phone.

"Somewhere around the place. He putters. Do all men putter, Mr. Archer? Do you putter?"

I let the curve go by. "We ought to find him and tell him about his brother."

"It shouldn't be hard to find him. Jerry never goes anywhere. Coming, Milly?"

"I don't feel very well." The girl looked badly wilted from the strain. Her dark head drooped on the white stalk of her neck.

"Will you be all right here?" I said.

"Of course I will. I'll keep a lookout for Carl."

"He won't be here for a while, unless he has a car."

"He may have, though. He may have stolen one. I think he drove away from Dr. Grantland's."

"Did you see him?"

"No. But I heard an engine start up just after he ran out."

"That's bad."

"Nothing good ever happens," Zinnia said. "Not to this precious family, anyway."

She put on a wide-brimmed Mexican straw hat, and we went out into the sun. It struck me like a slap across the eyes.

She led me around the side of the adobe. "Jerry's probably in his greenhouse. Flowers, he grows. Cymbidiums. He's got a green thumb that goes all the way up to his armpit. Well, I suppose everybody's got to be good at something."

In the narrow breezeway between the house and the garages, she suddenly turned to face me. Under the white shirt, her breasts were sharp and aggressive. "What are you good at, Mr. Archer?"

"Investigation."

"What kind of investigation?" Her intent hot face gave the question a double meaning.

I assumed both meanings. "I gather evidence in divorce cases, for example."

"Do you ever provide that kind of evidence personally?"

"Not when I'm conscious," I said. "I'm conscious now, in case it doesn't show."

"Oh but it does. What a pity. You're kind of cute in an ugly way, you know."

"You can have that compliment back if you want it, in spades."

That didn't faze her. She said: "Why don't you come back some time, minus bleeding-heart Milly? I still owe you a drink."

"I like to buy my own drinks."

"Oh? Are you loaded? I am."

"You're very flattering, Mrs. Heller." I wouldn't have touched the body coiled in my path with a forked stick, but it wouldn't have been tactful to say so. "What about Mr. Heller?"

"What about him? Don't ask me." She shrugged her shoulders. "Ask his damn cymbidiums. They know him better than I do."

"I don't know the language of the flowers, and we're wasting time."

"So what? There's plenty of time. Time is what hangs heavy on my hands." She raised her hands, turning them slowly on their slender wrists. "Pretty?"

"I've seen prettier."

Her eyes hardened, gleaming like chips of copper ore in the shadow of her hat. "What language do you speak?"

"You wouldn't know it."

"Don't you like women?"

"Women," I said, "I like. I have my own definition."

"God damn you." She leaned towards me, almost falling. I

held her up. Her teeth nicked my chin, and her mouth moved like a small hot animal under my ear. Her hat fell off.

I pushed her away, partly because she was another man's wife and partly because the other man was standing at the rear end of the breezeway, watching us. He had a pair of garden shears in his hand, which gleamed like a double dagger.

I picked up Zinnia's hat and handed it to her. "Calm yourself, blondie," I whispered. "Here's the cymbidium king."

She whispered back. "Did he see us?"

"Ask the cymbidiums."

He moved towards us, an older, smaller, heavier version of his brother. His coloring was similar, red hair and pink comlexion. It was his eyes that made the difference. They were sane, cynically and wearily sane. I looked down at the shears in his hand. He had a firm grip on them, and they were pointed at the middle of my body.

"Out," he said. "Get out."

"You don't know who I am."

"I don't care who you are. If you don't want to be gelded, get off my property and stay off my property. That includes my wife."

She was standing flat against the adobe wall, holding the hat in front of her like a flimsy shield. "Take it easy now, Jerry. I got something in my eye. This gentleman was trying to remove it."

He stood with his short legs planted wide apart, peering at me out of pale eyes. Their whites were yellowish from some internal complaint: bad digestion or bad conscience. "Is that how he got the lipstick on his face?"

"He didn't get it from me." But her hand went to her mouth.

"Who did he get it from then?"

"From Milly, probably. They came up here together. She's in the house now."

"You're a liar, Zinnia. You always have been a liar. It's a

wonder you're not better at it with all that practice."

"I'm not lying. Milly is in the house."

He turned to me. "Are you a friend of Milly's?"

"I suppose I am."

"He's a detective," Zinnia said. "She hired him."

"What for?"

He looked from one to the other of us, still holding the shears rigid in his hand.

"Carl's out of the asylum. He's got a gun, and he's threatening to kill you."

His face turned blotchy white. "Is Carl here now?" The words whistled in his throat.

"She thinks he's on his way."

"What else did she say?"

"Nothing else. Talk to her yourself." She went on the offensive suddenly: "You always used to like to talk to her. Didn't you? Which reminds me you've got your nerve accusing me of playing around, after all I've got on you."

He brushed the quarrel aside with a weary gesture. "You've been drinking again, Zinnia. You promised me you wouldn't drink in the daytime."

"Did I?"

"A dozen times."

"This was a special occasion."

"Why? Because you think that Carl is going to shoot me? Were you celebrating ahead of time?"

"You're crazy."

"Sure. Sure. I don't suppose you even called the police."

"Naturally I did. Jake Ostervelt's on his way out."

"Well. That's something, anyway." He turned to me. "Then we won't be needing you, will we, Mr. Detective?"

"I hope not," I said.

"I'm telling you we don't need you." He huffed and bristled, trying to recapture his anger, without success. His voice was dead: "So you get off my property like I said. This place belongs to me and as long as I'm alive and kicking I don't need any L.A. sharpie to look out for me *or* my wife."

"All right." There wasn't any other answer.

I went back to my car and drove towards Citrus Junction. A couple of miles from the Heller ranch, I passed a radio car headed in the opposite direction. It had two uniformed men in the front seat, and it was burning the asphalt.

The windowless packing plants of the lemon growers' co-operatives were major landmarks on the outskirts of town. The highway became the main street of the business section, which was composed of one new hotel and several old ones, bars and chain stores, a Sears, a giant drugstore whose architect had been inspired by hashish, four new-car agencies, three banks, and a couple of movie houses, one for *bracero* field-hands.

It was a slow town, clogged with money, stunned by sun. I made inquiries for Mr. Parish. His office was over the Mexican movie house. The stairs were as dark as a tunnel after the barren brilliance of the street. I groped my way along a second-floor corridor and through a battered door into a waiting room. Its sagging furniture and outdated magazines might have belonged to an old-fashioned dentist with a lower-income practice. An odor of fear and hopelessness hung in the air like a subtle gas.

An inner door opened. A young man appeared in the doorway. He had soft brown eyes, hardened by spectacles. He wore a threadbare tweed jacket patched with suede at the elbows, and a very cheerful smile. In my mood, an offensively cheerful smile.

"Dr. Parish?"

"Not doctor, thanks, though I'm working on my doctorate." He looked at me with professional solicitude, still smiling. "You've been referred to me? May I have your name?"

"Lew Archer."

"Sorry, I don't recall it. Should I have your file?"

"I'm not a patient," I said, "though I'm keeping my fingers crossed. I'm a private detective."

"Oh. Sorry." He seemed to be disappointed in a flustered, sensitive way. "Won't you come in?"

He seated me in a cubbyhole of an office containing two chairs, a desk, a grim green filing cabinet. There were holes in the uncarpeted floor where I guessed a dentist's chair had once been bolted. Under the floor, a remote passionate voice was declaiming in Spanish. I caught the words for love and death. *Amor. Morte.*

"It's the matinee in the theater downstairs. I hope it doesn't disturb you." He sat behind the desk and began to knock out a pipe in a brass ashtray. "Has one of my people got into some kind of trouble?" he said between the pipe-banging and the Spanish.

"Your people?"

"My clients. Actually they're more like a family to me. I think of them as my family, the whole hundred and fifty of them. They make a fairly hectic family group on occasion." He paused, filling his pipe. "Well, let's have the bad news. I can see bad news on your face. Is it klepto trouble again?"

"That enters into it, probably. He's carrying a gun, and they didn't give it to him as a going-away present from Mendocino."

"Just who are we talking about?"

"Carl Heller. Remember him?"

"I ought to. You don't mean to tell me they let him out?"

"I mean he escaped. He got to Los Angeles somehow, and turned up at my office this morning. Some friend of his at the institution had given him my name. Some enemy of mine."

"You saw Carl, then? How is he?" He leaned across the desk in boyish eagerness, tinged with anxiety.

"In bad condition, I'd say. I not only saw him, I also felt him."

I lifted my chin to show him the bruise on my neck.

Parish clucked with his tongue, irritatingly. "Carl's violent, eh? Too bad. How was his orientation?"

"If you mean is he off the rails, the answer is yes. I've seen paranoia before and he has the symptoms."

"Delusions of persecution?"

"He's full of 'em. Everybody's against him, including the cops. He seems to have delusions of grandeur, too. Claims he's the rightful heir to a million dollars."

Parish said softly through smoke: "Maybe he is at that. Oh, he's paranoid all right, I don't know how extreme — haven't seen him for years. He may also be rightful heir to a million dollars."

"You're kidding."

"I never kid about my people."

"Where would he get a million?"

"He didn't. That's the point. I can't help feeling he was cheated out of it, in a way. His father meant him to have half the estate. Of course Carl wasn't fit to handle it. Old Heller left the whole thing to his other son Jerry, with the understanding that he would provide for Carl. Then when the accident happened —"

"The old man's murder, you mean?"

"Accident," he said sharply. "Murder involves willful intention and knowledge of what you're doing. If Carl killed his father, he didn't know what he was doing. He was morally and legally not guilty."

"By reason of insanity."

"Of course. As it happened, the case never came to trial, and he was never convicted of anything worse than mental illness. But Jerry, his older brother —"

"I know Jerry. I went out to his ranch to offer him protection. He kicked me off the place. He had a wild idea that I was making advances to his wife. I hate to say this, but it was the other way around."

"Typical behavior from both of them. He's terribly jealous, and she gives him plenty of cause." He smiled with reminiscent grimness. "I was going to say, when I was interrupted, that Jerry took advantage of the tragic situation. As you probably know if you're a detective, there's a legal tradition which forbids a murderer to profit from his victim's death. Jerry shipped Carl off to Mendocino, and kept the whole estate for himself."

"And the estate is really worth a million dollars?"

"Double that. The old man bought up thousands of acres of lemon land during the depression. The family's much wealthier than you'd think from the way they live."

"You said an interesting thing a minute ago, Mr. Parish. You said *if* Carl killed his father. Is there any doubt that he did?"

"It was never proved. It was simply assumed."

"I thought he was caught in the act."

"That was his brother's statement to the coroner's jury. I tried to get the sheriff, who is also the coroner — I tried to get him to let me cross-examine Jerry Heller. He wouldn't permit it. I was new in my job, and that afternoon's work almost got me fired."

"You think Jerry was lying."

"Don't jump to conclusions. It's my job, as I see it, to keep people out of Mendocino, unless they're proven dangerous. If we sent away everyone with a paranoid streak, and locked them up for what amounts to life, the mental hospitals wouldn't begin to hold them."

"What about the cemeteries?" I said. "They'd soon be overflowing if we let all the Carl Hellers run around loose."

"I wonder. Carl was in pretty good shape when they let him out five years ago. Naturally the accident upset him again, threw him back into illness. It made him look very bad. He was tried in the court of public opinion and found guilty of homicidal mania. But I'm not completely convinced that he killed his father. He told me himself that the old man was lying dead when he entered the room. Then Jerry came in and caught him leaning over the bed, trying to untie the rope from his father's neck."

"Did Jerry frame him, in your opinion?"

"Please. I didn't say that. Carl may have killed him. Or Jerry may have believed that he did, sincerely. A million dollars can be a powerful motive for believing something. Myself, I've never known Carl to be really dangerous."

"He was this morning."

"Perhaps. After five years behind the walls. I'd like to see him for myself."

"You're a braver man than I am."

"I know him better than you. I like Carl."

"Evidently. But if he didn't kill his father, who did?"

"There were other people in the house. The servants had no reason to love old Heller. Neither had Jerry or Zinnia, for that matter. Sheriff Ostervelt was there, too, eating Thanksgiving dinner with the family. He's Heller's brother-in-law, and the old man owned him lock, stock and barrel." He caught himself up short, and his brown eyes veiled themselves behind the spectacles. "For heaven's sake, don't quote me to anyone. I'm a public employee, you know, and the Heller family has political pull."

"All this is off the record then?"

"I'm afraid it has to be, though I'd dearly like to do something for Carl and Mildred."

"The best thing we can do for him is find him before he hurts somebody."

"Yes. Of course. I agree."

The telephone on his desk rang jarringly. He picked it up and identified himself. I watched his brown eyes grow round and glassy.

"This is dreadful," he said. "Dreadful." He bit his lip. "Yes, I'll come right out. It happens that Mr. Archer is here with me.

Of course, Sheriff. I'll bring him along."

He set the receiver down, fumblingly, and ran his fingers through his thinning hair.

"Somebody else has been killed," I said.

"Yes. Jerry Heller. Shot in his greenhouse. They have the gun."

I murdered scores of insects on the ten-mile stretch of road between the town and the ranch. Parish sat beside me, watching the speedometer and gripping the door-handle. "This is dreadful, dreadful," he kept repeating.

We found Jerry Heller lying peacefully in the center aisle of his greenhouse. Cymbidium sprays in most of the colors of the rainbow, and some others, made a fine funeral display. The light fell muted through the transparent roof onto his dead face. A round red hole in his forehead made him appear three-eyed.

A big man in a wide-brimmed hat got up from a bench in one of the side aisles. He had a pitted nose and little uneasy eyes. His belly moved ahead of him down the aisle.

"Looks like your boy has gone and done it again," he said to Parish.

"It appears so, Sheriff." Parish was still upset, his voice high and wavering. But he stuck to his guns: "This time I hope you'll conduct a decent investigation, anyway."

"Investigation, hell. We know who killed Jerry. We know the motive. We got the weapon, even. It was stuck down in the dirt under one of these plants." He stepped over the body, heavily, and pointed at a ragged hole in the peat-moss. "All we got to do now is find him. You know his habits, don't you?"

"I knew Carl five years ago."

"He hasn't changed much, has he? Where do you think he is?"

"I haven't any idea." Parish looked up into the filtered light. "Hiding on the ranch?"

"It's possible. I'm having a posse formed. I want you to go

along with them. You can talk to him better than I can. He may have another gun, and we don't want any more killings."

"I'll be glad to," Parish said.

"Go and report to Deputy Santee, then. He's in the house telephoning." Parish went through an inner door which led through a covered passageway into the house. Before he closed it behind him, I caught a glimpse of Zinnia standing in the shadows of the passageway.

The sheriff turned a fish eye on me. "You Archer?"

"That's my name."

"I'm Ostervelt, the sheriff of this county. Remember that and we'll get along just fine. Mrs. Heller, Mildred that is, tells me you saw him this morning."

"He came to my office to try and hire me."

"What for?"

"Apparently he thought that he'd been framed —"

"He wasn't," Ostervelt said. "If you need any proof, look down at what's in front of you."

"I have."

"A nice piece of work, isn't it? Why in God's name didn't you grab him this morning and hold onto him?"

"I tried to. He got the drop on me."

"He wouldn't of got it on me. I'm older and fatter than you, but he wouldn't of got it on me." By way of illustration, he flung his suitcoat back and reached for his hip. A service forty-five hopped up in his hand. He thrust it back in its holster, smiling sleepily with rubbery lips. "You saw his gun?"

"Yes."

"Can you identify it?"

"I should be able to."

"Wait here, then. I'll go get it."

He went outside. As soon as the sound of his footsteps had receded, Zinnia Heller came out of the passageway. Her face was carved from chalk, but her pull-taffy hair was lacquered smooth and trim, with not a curl out of place. She stopped about ten feet short of the body, as if she'd come up against an invisible barrier. The long black butt of a target pistol protruded from the waistband of her slacks.

"Congratulations," I said.

"What do you mean?"

I moved towards her, sidestepping her defunct mate. "You're really loaded now."

"You mustn't talk like that." Genuine anguish, or something very like it, pulled downwards at her mouth. "Okay, so we weren't a perfect married couple. That doesn't make me glad the poor guy got killed."

"Two million dollars should."

"Who have you been talking to?"

"The flowers," I said. "The flowers and the birds."

She took hold of my coatsleeve. "Listen. I wanted to ask you a favor. Don't tell them that we quarreled before he died."

"Why? Did you shoot him?"

"Don't be crazy."

"I'm not. Everybody else seems to be. But I'm not."

"It just wouldn't look right," she said. "It might make them suspicious. Ostervelt has a down on me, anyway. He was married to the old man's sister, and he always thought he should have a piece of the property. We did enough for him already, canceling his debts."

"You canceled his debts?"

"Jerry did, after the old man died."

"Why would Jerry do that?"

"He did it out of pure generosity, not that it's any of your business. You make me sick with your suspicions. You're suspicious of everybody."

"Including you," I said.

"You are crazy. And I was a fool to try and talk to you."

"Talk some more. How did this happen?"

"I wasn't present, is that clear? I didn't even hear the shot."

"Where were you?"

"Taking a shower, if you want to know."

"Can you prove it?"

"Examine me. I'm clean." Her green eyes flashed with never-say-die eroticism.

I backed away. "Where was the sheriff?"

"Searching the stables. He thought maybe Carl was there. Carl used to spend a lot of time in the stables."

"Has he been seen at all?"

"Not to my knowledge. If I do see him, you'll know it. So will he." She patted the target-pistol stuck in her waistband.

Returning footsteps crackled in the gravel. She smoothed her face and tried to look like a widow. She went on looking like exactly what she was: a hard blonde beauty in her fading thirties, fighting the world with two weapons, sex and money. Both of her weapons had turned in her hands and scarred her.

The sheriff entered the greenish gloom, with Mildred trailing reluctantly at his heels. She was pale and anxious-eyed. When I approached her, she looked down at the packed earth floor of the greenhouse. Her mouth trembled into speech:

"It wasn't any use after all. Why did you go away?"

"I was forced to. Your brother-in-law ordered me off the ranch. He must have been shot within a few minutes after that."

"Did Carl really do it, do you think?"

"That's the idea the sheriff is trying to sell. I haven't taken an option on it yet."

She raised her eyes from the brown earth, and managed a small grateful smile. Sheriff Ostervelt tapped my shoulder. "Here. I want to show you."

He had a black enameled evidence case in his hands. He carried it as if it was full of jewels. Setting it down on a bench, he unlocked it and opened it, with the air of a magician. It contained a .32-caliber Smith and Wesson nickel-plated revolver — the gun that Carl had flourished in my office.

"Don't touch it," Ostervelt said. "I can't see any prints with the naked eye, but I'm going to have it tested for latent ones. Is this the gun that Heller pulled on you?"

"That one or its twin."

"You're sure about that? You know guns?"

"Yes. But you still haven't proved it fired the shot that killed Jerry Heller. Where's the slug?"

"Still in his head. Don't worry, I intend to run ballistics tests. Not that it ain't wrapped up already. This revolver was left at the scene of the crime with one shell empty that had just been fired."

"How do you know it had just been fired?"

"I smelled it. Smell it yourself."

I leaned down and caught the acrid odor of recently expended smokeless powder. Mildred, who had been standing in the background with Zinnia, moved up behind me. Looking down into the black metal box, she let out an exclamation of surprise and dismay.

"What's the trouble, Milly?" Ostervelt said.

She didn't answer for what seemed a long time. She looked at him and then at me, her mouth drooping dismally.

"What is it?" he repeated. "If you know something, speak up."

"I've seen that gun before. I think I have, anyway."

"Does it belong to Carl?"

"No. It's Dr. Grantland's. My employer in Beverly Hills. It looks exactly the same as the one in his desk."

"How did it get here, then?"

"I haven't any idea," she answered faintly.

"Wait a minute," I said. "You told me Carl rifled his cash drawer this morning. Did the doctor keep his revolver in the same drawer?"

"I think he did. I've seen it there. I couldn't swear that it's the same revolver."

Zinnia pushed forward between us, her sharp elbow jabbing my side. "Maybe you better talk to Bobby Grantland."

"Do you know him?"

"I ought to. He's spent enough weekends here. He and Jerry went to school together."

I turned to Mildred. "Didn't you say Grantland was Carl's psychiatrist?"

"He was for a while after the war. That's why he gave me a job, I guess."

Zinnia snorted. "Like hell it is. Jerry got you that job with Bobby Grantland. Now that Jerry's dead, it's time you showed a little gratitude for all he's done for you."

"Gratitude for what?" Mildred turned on her in a thin white fury. "For giving me a chance to go to work for fifty dollars a week?"

"He sent you money as long as you needed it, didn't he?"

"He sent me a little money, for a while. *You* put a stop to that."

"You're right. I did. There's no reason why he had to support every female bum that married into the family."

"He supported you," Mildred said. "Speaking of female bums. You've got it all to yourself now. Aren't you satisfied?"

They were on the verge of hair-pulling. Zinnia reached for her. I put a hand on her arm, and she drew back. The sheriff's little eyes squinted stupidly at us, as if the quick turn of events had befuddled his brain. Mildred backed away and stood against a raised planter, plucking idly at the tiny shell-like blossoms on a young cymbidium spray.

"Let me get this straight," Ostervelt said. "You said something just now, Zinnia, that Jerry made the doc give Milly a job. How could Jerry do that?"

"Bobby Grantland owed him money, that's how. Jerry lent

him the capital to set up in practice after the war."

"Does he still owe him the money?"

"I guess so, most of it. I think he's been paying it back a little at a time."

"Was Jerry pressing him for it?"

"I wouldn't know. Ask him."

I said: "Was Grantland here five years ago? The day that old Mr. Heller was strangled?"

Mildred answered: "Yes, he was. He came up to observe Carl. But this is ridiculous. He couldn't have had anything to do with any of this."

"Did he testify at Carl's sanity hearing?"

"Of course he did."

"What did he say about Carl?"

"I don't know. I wasn't there. I couldn't face it."

"I was," Zinnia said. "I don't remember the two-dollar words, but they added up to the fact that my esteemed brother-in-law was as nutty as a fruitcake. Was and is."

"Maybe. I'd like to talk to the good doctor, about that and other things."

"Me, too." Sheriff Ostervelt snapped his black case shut and tucked it under his hamlike arm. He went to Mildred, walking like a bear on its hind legs, and laid a large red paw on her shoulder. "Coming along with me, little girl?"

She shrank at his touch. "I'll ride with Mr. Archer. He brought me here."

"Now don't be like that." His hand slid round her shoulders in a gesture that was more than paternal. "I'd enjoy your company, Mildred. Besides, I need you to show me the way. I'm just an old hick from the sticks. I don't know those Los Angeles streets the way he does. Of course I got to admit I'm not as young and pretty as he is."

His belly nudged her. She leaned away from him against the plants. "I'll go with you if you don't touch me," she said in a tiny voice. "Promise that you won't touch me."

"Sure. Of course." He took a backward step and said with jovial lechery: "You got me wrong, Mildred. You never understood me. I wouldn't hurt a hair on your little head. And nobody else is going to, either, not while you got old Ostie to protect you."

They left the greenhouse together. Mildred dragged her feet. The sheriff turned at the door and cocked his chins at me. "You coming, Archer?"

"In a minute. I'll follow your car."

When they were out of earshot, Zinnia said: "A pretty couple, eh? I'd like to see the old goat marry her. She's just what he deserves."

"I thought he was married, to your father-in-law's sister."

"He was. She died before the old man did. Ostie never got over it."

"I can see that. He's the typical grief-stricken widower."

"Oh sure. I mean he never got over her dying before the old man. It cut him off from any part of the estate. Personally, I think he did all right for himself, getting Jerry to wipe out all he owed him."

"How much?"

"I wouldn't know. Ten thousand dollars or more."

"For services rendered?"

Her eyes narrowed. "Are you back on that kick again? You make me tired."

"The sheriff helped to send Carl up, didn't he? That could have been worth a lot of money to Jerry."

"Nuts," she said. "You're completely off the beam. Maybe Ostie did want Carl out of the way, but if he did it had nothing to do with Jerry. Ostie's been after Milly to divorce Carl and marry him for a long time."

"He hasn't been very successful in his wooing."

"No." She laughed raucously, like a parrot. "Well, climb on

your horse, big boy. Don't let me keep you."

"Why don't you come along?"

"So I can listen to you some more, telling me how Jerry framed his brother? No, thanks." She turned and looked at the body. "This little guy wasn't much use to me, but he had his points. I'll stay here with him."

"Are you all right by yourself?"

"I won't be by myself. There's a deputy inside" — she jerked a thumb towards the passageway that led into the house — "and more on the way. What's the matter, can't you make up your mind? A minute ago Carl was framed, to hear you tell it. Now he's a lurking menace again. Come on now, which is it."

"I don't know," I said. "You're right. I haven't made up my mind."

I left her keeping her unlikely vigil. Looking back from outside, I saw her hefting the light target-pistol in her hand. She waved it at me derisively.

The sheriff drove inconsistently, slowing gradually on the long dull straightaways and speeding up on the curves. I was tempted to pass him more than once, but I wanted to keep an eye on him and the girl. She sat on the extreme righthand side of the front seat, as if to avoid any possible contact with him.

I followed his undercover plates over the Pass, down Sunset and across to Santa Monica Boulevard. He parked eventually on a side street near the center of Beverly Hills. I parked behind his radio car and got out.

Ostervelt and Mildred went up a flagstone walk which led to a low pink building standing well back from the street. It was flat-roofed and new-looking, walled with glass bricks in front and masked with well-clipped shrubbery. A small bronze plate on the doorpost announced discreetly: J. Robert Grantland, M.D.

I followed them into a bright waiting room furnished in net and black iron. A receptionist's desk was set at an angle in one corner. There were several abstract paintings on the walls. I touched one and felt the brushmarks. Originals. Everything about the place said money, but meant front.

Mildred opened a heavy white door. We went through into a smaller room furnished with white oak office furniture. I pointed at the wide low telephone desk against one wall:

"Is this the desk he took the money from?"

She had assumed a professional mask as soon as she entered the office. "Yes. Please keep your voice down. I think the doctor has a patient with him."

I listened, and heard a drone of voices behind an inner door. One of them was a woman's. It said:

"Is that why I fall in love with Terry's friends?"

A lower voice, as rich and thick as molasses, answered her. I couldn't hear what it said.

"Break it up, will you, Milly?" the sheriff said. "We can't wait here all day."

She looked at him primly, her finger to her lips. "Dr. Grantland hates to be interrupted. And promise me you won't say anything nasty to him. He couldn't help it if Carl took his gun."

The sheriff grunted. "We'll see." He put his evidence case on top of the desk and pulled out the top drawer.

Looking over his shoulder, I saw that it was empty, except for a little silver in a coin compartment at one end, and, shoved far back in the drawer, a carton of .32 shells.

"Is this where the gun was kept?"

"I think so. I've seen it there."

"What was Grantland doing with a gun?"

"I don't know. I never asked him. Some of his patients get pretty — excited sometimes. I suppose he kept it for protection."

There were footsteps in the inner room. The door clicked sharply, and opened. A heavy man in English tweeds came out. The artificial light gleamed on his head, which was prematurely bald, and flashed on his spectacles.

"What is this, Mrs. Heller? Who are these men?"

She cringed and stammered. Ostervelt answered for her:

"Remember me, Doctor? Jack Ostervelt, sheriff of Buena County. We met at the Heller place a couple of times."

"Sure enough, we did. How are you, Sheriff?"

He closed the door behind him, but not before I caught a glimpse of a dark-haired woman with a raddled face, putting on a hat.

"I'm well enough myself. Your friend Jerry Heller is pretty poorly, though. In fact he's dead."

"Jerry dead?" The doctor's jaw dropped so far I could see the gold in his molars.

"He was killed with this gun a couple of hours ago." The sheriff opened his black box. "Take a good look, but don't touch it. Recognize it?"

"Why, it looks like my revolver."

"That's what I thought," Ostervelt said flatly.

"Surely you don't imagine that I shot Jerry?" The doctor glanced anxiously at the door behind him, and lowered his voice with an effort. "My revolver was taken from my desk this morning. I reported it stolen to the police."

"Who stole it?"

He looked at Mildred. Her gaze met his, and dropped. Her face was miserable.

"Carl Heller did," he said. "He also took about fifty dollars in cash, which I kept in the same drawer."

I said: "Do you know for a fact that he took your gun?"

His fat chest pouted out, and he looked at me with hostility. "You can take my word for it. Just who are you, by the way?"

"The name is Archer," I said. "Have you been here all day, Doctor?"

"Certainly I have."

"Can you prove it?"

"Of course I can. Mrs. Monaco has been here with me for the past two hours, if you insist on proof."

"That won't be necessary," Ostervelt said. "You're absolutely certain that Carl Heller took your gun?"

Grantland's face flushed. "This is ridiculous. Of course I am. I saw him run out of here with the gun in his hand. I did my best to stop him, but he was too fast for me." He turned to Mildred. "You saw him, didn't you?"

"I guess so," she said hopelessly. "Yes, I saw him."

Her body began to slump. Thinking that she was going to faint, I started for her. Ostervelt got to her first, circling her slender body with his arm. She leaned against him, with her eyelids fluttering.

Dr. Grantland brought her a glass of water. "You'd better go home, Mrs. Heller. You've been under quite a strain. You need a rest."

"Yes." Her voice was like a tired little girl's.

"I'll take her," Ostervelt said. "Be glad to. With that crazy husband of hers still on the loose, she needs somebody to look out for her."

Grantland looked him up and down, sardonically. "No doubt."

"Sorry to bother you, Doctor. I guess when it comes to trial, we'll be needing you as a witness."

Ostervelt closed the evidence case and picked it up in one huge hand. He and Mildred went out, his thick possessive arm still supporting her. Grantland said to me:

"Is there something else?"

"Just a little matter of your professional opinion. It's been suggested to me that Carl Heller wasn't really dangerous."

"I thought so myself at one time. Obviously he is, though. He's killed two people, and the proof of the pudding is always in the eating."

"I don't quite follow."

"No, I suppose not. You wouldn't." He looked at me with intellectual distaste. "I'll spell it out for you. Five or six years ago I formed the opinion, based on observation and interviews, that Carl Heller wasn't likely to become dangerous. He was ill, of course, no question about that — definitely a victim of paranoid schizophrenia. But shock therapy seemed to do him a lot of good. He was released from the state hospital, not as cured, you understand, but as an arrested case, who needed supportive treatment. Schizophrenia isn't really curable, you know. We psychiatrists hate to admit failure, but that's the simple truth. Still, I concurred in the institution's fairly hopeful prognosis, and I was glad to see him let out on indefinite leave of absence."

"This was before his father was killed?"

"Of course. His father's death naturally altered my opinion. When theory collides with fact, you change the theory."

"I understand you were in the house that day?"

"I was. I drove up to see Carl, and the family asked me to stay for Thanksgiving dinner. Jerry and I are old friends."

"So Zinnia said —"

"Oh. You've been talking to Zinnia. What else did she say?"

"She mentioned that you owed money to Jerry Heller."

"Zinnia would. But she's a little behind the times. I paid Jerry off in full last year." His eyes glinted ironically behind the spectacles. "So if you're looking for a motive for murder, you'll have to look elsewhere. Now if you'll excuse me, I have work to do."

"Just a minute, doctor. Why did you give Mildred Heller a job?"

"Why not? I needed a receptionist, and she's a pleasant little creature. I suppose I felt sorry for her. Besides, Jerry asked me to. I had a number of reasons."

"What were his reasons?"

"For finding her a job? No doubt he felt he should do something for her. Zinnia made him cut off her allowance, and she had to live somehow."

"On fifty dollars a week."

He said with some complacency: "I've been paying her sixty since the first of the year."

"Don't you feel she got a pretty lousy deal from Jerry?"

"I've always thought so, yes, though I didn't blame Jerry entirely. Zinnia ran him since his father died."

"How did she get along with the old man before he died?"

"Not too well, I'm afraid. None of them did. He was a German patriarch, a hard-fisted domineering old curmudgeon. A typical arthritic."

"You know the family better than I do, Doctor. Could Zinnia have killed him?"

"Do you mean is it morally possible? Or physically possible?"

"Both."

"I thought Jerry was your suspect."

"He still is. They both are."

"Well, as far as physical possibility is concerned, either one of them could have strangled him. He was helpless with his arthritis, and alone. His room was accessible to all of them, and the family was scattered that evening. Jerry was in his greenhouse, I believe, but there's a passage from it directly into the house. I don't really know where Zinnia was. She said later that she was taking a walk."

"And Ostervelt?"

"The sheriff left early, I think, before it happened. He got drunk at dinner and made some kind of a pass at Mildred. She slapped his face and stomped off to her room. That's how Carl happened to be left alone."

"Where were you?"

"I played a couple of hands of canasta with Carl. He lost, and quit. He was in an unpleasant mood, probably the aftermath of the trouble between Ostervelt and his wife. Anyway, he wandered off and I picked up a book. The next I saw or heard of him, he and Jerry were fighting in the old man's room. The old man was dead, and Jerry said he'd caught him *in flagrante*."

"But it could have been the other way around?"

"Not in view of what's happened since," he said.

"I don't know. Jerry profited from his father's death. Nobody else did. Zinnia profits from Jerry's, and nobody else does."

"You're suggesting that he killed his father, and then she turned around and killed him?"

"I'm saying it could have happened that way. Carl's escape may have been the opportunity she was waiting for."

"That's an ingenious story you've made up. But it doesn't fit the facts. Not if I know Zinnia, and I think I do. She's a hard-nosed bitch, but she wouldn't kill. And not if Jerry was shot with my revolver. There doesn't seem to be any question that Carl killed them both."

"Would you swear that he had your revolver?"

"How many times do I have to tell you?" He rapped the top of the white oak desk with his knuckles. "He took it out of the drawer in this desk. I saw him with my own eyes."

"So did I. At least I saw a nickel-plated revolver. Maybe it was your revolver and maybe it wasn't. Maybe it was the murder weapon and maybe it wasn't. It's interesting that Mildred didn't see him take it."

"She did, though. You heard her say so."

"A few minutes ago, she did. Not this morning. When she came to me this morning, she didn't even know he had a gun."

"On the contrary. She knew it very well. She was right here in this room with me. She saw him run out that door with the gun in his hand." He pointed at the closed white door of the waiting room. "She even pleaded with me not to call the police about it, but naturally I did, as soon as she left."

"That's not her story."

"Are you calling me a liar?"

"Somebody is a liar."

He took an awkward boxing stance and raised his balled fists. "I've taken enough from you. Now you get out of here or I'll throw you out."

"I wouldn't try it, Doctor. You look out of training. Just tell me where she lives, and I'll go peacefully. I want to check your stories against each other."

"Do that," he snapped. "She has an apartment in the Vista Hotel. Number 317. It's not far —"

"I know where it is, thanks."

I went out into the quiet residential street and got into my car. A sprinkler on the lawn across the street had caught a rainbow in its net of spray. Above the treetops in the distance, the tower of the city hall stood whitely against the sky, a symbol of law and order and prosperity. I kicked the starter savagely. Behind its peaceful façade, the afternoon was swollen with disaster. Like a monster struggling to be born out of the vast blue belly of the sky.

The Vista Hotel was an old three-story building which stood on a green triangle near the Boulevard. It was swept by waves of sound from the unceasing traffic. An iron fire escape wept long yellow tears down its stucco sides. I drove by slowly, looking for a parking place.

Above the sound of my engine, the remoter roar from the boulevard, something cracked in the air. I stopped my car and looked up at the sky. If it had split like an eggshell, I wouldn't have been surprised. But the sky was serene enough.

I left the car where it was, in the middle of the street. Before I reached the sidewalk, the cracking noise was repeated. Somebody said, "No," in a high voice which sounded barely human.

A man appeared on the hotel fire escape, outside a third-floor window. He hung over the railing for a moment, like a seasick passenger on a ship. His short hair shone like wheat stubble in the sun. His mouth was bright with blood.

He started down the fire escape, holding on to the railing, hand-over-hand. Ostervelt came out on the iron platform above him, his forty-five in his fist. He pointed it at Carl Heller's head and sighted along the barrel.

I shouted at the top of my lungs: "Don't shoot!"

Ostervelt was as oblivious as a statue. The flash of his gun was pale in the light, but in the open air the crack was louder. It sounded like something breaking, something valuable which could never be replaced.

Carl stood on the iron steps, leaning against the railing, perfectly still, as if he had been transfixed by a terrible insight. Anguish was radiant on his face. Then his head and his knees went loose, and he somersaulted to the second-floor platform. He lay there like a bundle of blue rags.

I climbed up to him. The drag of gravity was powerful on my legs. When I got to him he was dead. There was a hole in the back of his head, another hole in the middle of his back, a third hole in his belly. He was barefooted.

Above me, Ostervelt replaced his gun in its holster with the air of a good workman putting away a tool. He sat down heavily on the iron steps:

"Too bad. I had to do it. He was hiding in the kitchenette in Milly's apartment. I figure he was waiting until I left, so he could get his crazy hands on her. I heard a noise in there. I pulled my gun and opened the door. He came at me with a knife in his hand."

"Where's the knife?"

"He dropped it when I plugged him the first time. Dropped it and made for the window."

"Did you have to shoot him twice more?"

"Maybe not. I usually finish what I start. He wasn't much use to himself alive, anyway. You might say that I saved him a lot of grief."

"I think he had it all," I said. "All the grief there is."

"Maybe so. Well, it's all over now."

"Not quite." I looked down at the ruined head.

A prowl car rounded the corner and squealed to a stop behind my double-parked car. Two uniformed cops with outraged faces got out. Ostervelt yelled in a big cracked voice:

"Up here."

The men in uniform ran across the lawn towards the fire escape. Their feet were silent in the grass.

"You handle them, Sheriff," I said. "I want to talk to Mildred."

He rose with a sigh and stood against the wall to let me pass him on the narrow steps. I didn't want to touch him. But his belly protruded like a medicine ball under his clothes, and I had to.

Mildred's room was cheaply furnished with a studio bed, a threadbare rug, a couple of chairs, a record-player on a rickety table. The sheriff's evidence case was on the table beside it. Mildred was hunched over on the edge of the studio bed with her face in her hands. When I stepped over the windowsill, I saw her eyes sparkle between her fingers:

"Is he dead?"

"Ostervelt saw to that."

"How dreadful." She dropped her hands. Her face was white and intent. There were no tears on it. She said: "Yet I suppose it had to be. It's lucky for me that Ostie came up here with me. He might have killed me."

"I doubt that, Mrs. Heller."

"He killed the others," she said. "It would have been my turn next. You should have seen him when he came lunging out with that knife in his hand."

A long knife gleamed on the worn rug outside the open door to the kitchenette. I picked it up and tested its edge with my thumb. It was a wavy-edged bread-knife, very sharp. A few small bread crumbs clung to its shining surface.

"I wish I had been here," I said. "I'd have taken the knife away from him. Your husband would still be alive."

"You don't know what you're saying. He was terribly strong —"

"Not as strong as you, Mrs. Heller. He was like a child in your hands. So was I for a while."

"What do you mean?"

I didn't answer her. I turned on my heel and went into the kitchenette. It was a tiny cubicle containing an apartment stove and refrigerator, a sink and a small cupboard. A loaf of bread and an open jar of peanut butter stood on the masonite work-board beside the sink. A slice of bread, half-severed, hung on one end of the loaf. A pot of coffee was steaming on the stove.

On a towel-rack above the stove, a pair of grey cotton socks were hanging limply. I took them down and stretched them out in my hands. They were clean and very large, about size twelve — a pair of men's work socks which someone had washed and hung up to dry. They were nearly dry.

Mildred appeared in the doorway. Her blue eyes were inky, almost black in her white face:

"What are you doing in here? You've got no right to interfere with my things."

I held up the grey socks. "Are these your things? They're pretty big for you."

"What are they? How did they get here?"

"They're your husband's socks. He wore them here. Apparently he took them off and washed them and hung them up to dry. He must have done that quite some time ago, because they're just about dry. Feel them."

She backed away, her arms stiff at her sides.

"He must have been here in your apartment for quite a long time," I said. "In fact, I'll give you odds that Carl was here all day."

"But that's impossible. He was at the ranch. There was the gun."

"Yes, there was the gun. But there was no evidence that he carried it there or used it on his brother."

"I saw him there." Her face was grim and haggard, as if a generation of years had fallen on her in the past five minutes. "I went out in the greenhouse to see if Jerry was all right. Carl was with him. I actually saw him shoot Jerry."

"Where were you?"

"In the passageway between the house and the greenhouse."

"That much I believe."

"It's true. It's all true."

"Why didn't you tell us before?"

"I hated to. After all I am his wife."

"His widow," I said. "His merry little widow. You didn't tell us because it didn't happen. You went out in the greenhouse, no doubt, but Jerry was alone. And you were carrying the revolver yourself."

"I couldn't have," she said. "You know I couldn't have. Carl had the revolver. I saw him take it from Dr. Grantland's desk."

"Why didn't you tell me that this morning?"

"Didn't I? It must have slipped my mind. Anyway, he had it. He showed it to you in your office this morning. You told me that yourself."

"I know I did. Is that when you got your big idea?"

"What big idea? I don't understand."

"The big idea of shooting Jerry and using Carl's escape for a coverup. The same way you used him to cover you when you strangled his father."

Her breath was quick, and loud in the hidden passages of her head. "How did you know?"

"I didn't know for certain, until now."

"You tricked me." She spat the words.

"That's fair enough. You conned me nicely in my office this

morning. When I told you Carl was carrying a gun, you put on a very good act. Surprised alarm. It took me in completely. The gun was in your bag at that very moment. I suppose you met him coming out of my office, and talked him into giving you the gun. Talked him into coming here to your apartment and lying low. He was the sucker of the century, but I was a close second. I even gave you transportation to the scene of the crime. And you went through the same routine that worked five years ago, and almost worked again."

Her mouth twisted in a ghastly mimicry of a coaxing smile. "You wouldn't tell anybody on me, would you? You don't know what I've been through, how awful it was to marry a man and have him turn out crazy. And then we had to go and live with his family. You don't know how I suffered from that family. I thought if the old man died, we'd be able to get some money and break free. How was I to know they'd lock Carl up for it? Or that Jerry would cut me off the way he did?"

"Is that why you killed Jerry?"

"He deserved it. Besides, I was afraid they'd open the case again when Carl escaped."

"Did Carl deserve what you did to him?"

"I didn't do it," she said. "It was Sheriff Ostervelt."

"You set him up for Ostervelt. You knew he was here. You knew that Ostervelt was trigger-happy, and stuck on you besides. You brought him up here and sat and let it happen."

"Carl was no great loss to anybody. None of them was."

"They were human beings," I said. "Somebody has to pay for them."

Her face brightened. "I'll pay. I don't have a great deal, but Carl had several insurance policies. I'll go halves with you. Nobody has to know all this. Do they?"

"You've got me wrong. Money won't pay for lives."

"Listen to me," she said rapidly. "Twenty thousand dollars, that's what I'll give you. It's more than half of the insurance money that's coming to me."

"You've got more than that coming to you, Mrs. Heller. A private room made of concrete, without any windows."

She took in my meaning slowly. It hit her like a delayed-action bullet, disorganizing her face. She turned and ran across the living room. When I came out of the kitchenette, she had the black case open, the revolver in her hand like a silver forefinger pointed at my heart. It gleamed in the long shadow that fell across the room from the single window.

I glanced at the window. Ostervelt was there, his elbow propped on the sill. His forty-five roared and spat. Mildred took three steps backwards and slammed against the wall like a body dropped from a height. The blood gushed from her breast. She tried to hold it in with her fists. She said, "Ostie?" in a tone of girlish surprise. Then the rising blood gagged her.

She covered her mouth politely with her hand, and fell down dead. Ostervelt clambered awkwardly through the window. His face was solemn. His eyes were little and hard and dry.

"You didn't have to kill her, Sheriff. You could have shot the revolver out of her hand."

"I know I could."

"I thought you were fond of the girl."

"I was. I heard what you said about the gas chamber. I also heard what she said. It was cleaner this way." He was thoughtful for a minute, listening to the clatter of footsteps on the fire escape. "Anyway, she shouldn't have let me shoot Carl. I don't like that. It wasn't fair to him or to me. It wasn't fair to the law." He looked down at the heavy gun. "What did the crazy fella think he was doing, coming out like that with the knife in his hand?"

"He was cutting bread," I said. "He was going to make himself a peanut butter sandwich."

Ostervelt sighed deeply. Policemen started to come into the room.

# STRANGERS IN TOWN

*Strangers in Town: Three Newly Discovered Mysteries* by Ross Macdonald, edited by Tom Nolan, is printed on 60-pound Glatfelter Supple Opaque Natural (a recycled acid-free stock) from 12-point Century Schoolbook. The cover painting is by Deborah Miller. The first printing comprises four hundred copies sewn in cloth, signed and numbered by the editor (and including a facsimile of the author's signature), and approximately two thousand softcover copies. Each of the clothbound copies includes a separate pamphlet, *Winnipeg, 1929* by Ross Macdonald. The book was printed and bound by Thomson-Shore, Inc., Dexter, Michigan, and published in February 2001 by Crippen & Landru Publishers, Norfolk, Virginia.

# CRIPPEN & LANDRU, PUBLISHERS
## P. O. Box 9315
## Norfolk, VA 23505
## E-mail: CrippenL@Pilot.Infi.Net
## Web: www.crippenlandru.com

Crippen & Landru publishes first edition short-story collections by important detective and mystery writers. Most books are issued in two editions: trade softcover, and signed, limited clothbound with either a typescript page from the author's files or an additional story in a separate pamphlet. As of February 2001, the following books have been published:

*Speak of the Devil* by John Dickson Carr. 1994. Out of Print.

*The McCone Files* by Marcia Muller. 1995. Signed, limited clothbound, out of print; trade softcover, fifth printing, $15.00.

*The Darings of the Red Rose* by Margery Allingham. 1995. Out of Print.

*Diagnosis: Impossible, The Problems of Dr. Sam Hawthorne* by Edward D. Hoch. 1996. Signed, limited clothbound, out of print; softcover, 2nd printing, $15.00.

*Spadework: A Collection of "Nameless Detective" Stories* by Bill Pronzini. 1996. Signed, limited clothbound, out of print; signed overrun copies, $30.00; trade softcover, $16.00.

*Who Killed Father Christmas? And Other Unseasonable Demises* by Patricia Moyes. 1996. Signed, limited clothbound, $40.00; trade softcover, $16.00.

*My Mother, The Detective: The Complete "Mom" Short Stories*, by James Yaffe. 1997. Signed, limited clothbound, out of print; trade softcover, $15.00.

*In Kensington Gardens Once . . .* by H. R. F. Keating. 1997. Signed, limited clothbound, out of print; trade softcover, $12.00.

*Shoveling Smoke: Selected Mystery Stories* by Margaret Maron. 1997. Signed, limited clothbound, out of print; trade softcover, third printing, $16.00.

*The Man Who Hated Banks and Other Mysteries* by Michael Gilbert. 1997. Signed, limited clothbound, out of print; trade softcover, second printing, $16.00.

*The Ripper of Storyville and Other Ben Snow Tales* by Edward D. Hoch. 1997. Signed, limited clothbound, out of print; trade softcover, $16.00.

*Do Not Exceed the Stated Dose* by Peter Lovesey. 1998. Signed, limited clothbound, out of print; trade softcover, $16.00.

*Renowned Be Thy Grave; Or, The Murderous Miss Mooney* by P. M. Carlson. 1998. Signed, limited clothbound, out of print; trade softcover, $16.00.

*Carpenter and Quincannon, Professional Detective Services* by Bill Pronzini. 1998. Signed, limited clothbound, out of print; trade softcover, second printing, $16.00.

*Not Safe After Dark and Other Stories* by Peter Robinson. 1998. Signed, limited clothbound, out of print; trade softcover, second printing, $16.00.

*The Concise Cuddy, A Collection of John Francis Cuddy Stories* by Jeremiah Healy. 1998. Signed, limited clothbound, out of print; trade softcover, $17.00.

*One Night Stands* by Lawrence Block. 1999. Out of print.

*All Creatures Dark and Dangerous* by Doug Allyn. 1999. Signed, limited clothbound, out of print; trade softcover, $16.00.

*Famous Blue Raincoat: Mystery Stories* by Ed Gorman. 1999. Signed, limited clothbound, out of print; signed overrun copies, $30.00; trade softcover, $17.00.

*The Tragedy of Errors and Others* by Ellery Queen. 1999. Limited clothbound, out of print; trade softcover, second printing, $16.00.

*McCone and Friends* by Marcia Muller. 2000. Signed, limited clothbound, out of print; trade softcover, $16.00.

*Challenge the Widow Maker and Other Stories of People in Peril* by Clark Howard. 2000. Signed, limited clothbound, out of print; trade softcover, $16.00.

*The Velvet Touch* by Edward D. Hoch. 2000. Signed, limited clothbound, out of print; trade softcover, $16.00.

*Fortune's World* by Michael Collins. 2000. Signed, limited clothbound, out of print; trade softcover, $16.00.

*Tales Out of School: Mystery Stories* by Carolyn Wheat. 2000. Signed, limited clothbound, $40.00; trade softcover, $16.00.

*Long Live the Dead: Tales from Black Mask* by Hugh B. Cave. 2000. Signed, limited clothbound, out of print; trade softcover, $16.00.

*Stakeout on Page Street and Other DKA Files* by Joe Gores. 2000. Signed, limited clothbound, out of print; signed overrun copies, $30.00; trade softcover, $16.00.

*Strangers in Town: Three Newly Discovered Mysteries* by Ross Macdonald, edited by Tom Nolan. 2001. Limited clothbound, $37.00; trade softcover, $15.00.

## Forthcoming Short-Story Collections

*The Celestial Buffet* by Susan Dunlap.
*Adam and Eve on a Raft: Mystery Stories* by Ron Goulart.
*Kisses of Death: Nate Heller Stories* by Max Allan Collins.
*One Night Stands* by Lawrence Block (2nd edition, enlarged).
*The Old Spies Club and Other Intrigues of Rand* by Edward D. Hoch.
*The Reluctant Detective and Other Stories* by Michael Z. Lewin.
*Jo Gar's Casebook* by Raoul Whitfield.
*The 13 Culprits* by Georges Simenon, translated by Peter Schulman.
*Nine Sons and Other Mysteries* by Wendy Hornsby.
*The Dark Snow and Other Stories* by Brendan DuBois.
*The Adventure of the Murdered Moths and Other Radio Mysteries* by Ellery Queen.
*Problems Solved* by Bill Pronzini and Barry N. Malzberg.
*Kill the Umpire: The Calls of Ed Gorgon* by Jon L. Breen.
*The Spotted Cat and Other Mysteries: The Casebook of Inspector Cockrill* by Christianna Brand.
*One of a Kind: Collected Mystery Stories* by Eric Wright.
*Cuddy Plus One* by Jeremiah Healy.
*What Happened at Castelbonato* by Michael Gilbert.
*The Iron Angel and Other Tales of Michael Vlado* by Edward D. Hoch.
[Untitled Slot-Machine Kelly collection] by Michael Collins.
[Untitled collection from *Detective Fiction Weekly*] by Hugh B. Cave.

Crippen & Landru offers discounts to individuals and institutions who place Standing Order Subscriptions for all its forthcoming publications. Please write or e-mail for details.